FLOMMY THE ROBOT

PART ONE

ATTACK OF THE ROBOT PLANET

DANIEL ROBINSON

An ETHERGUN PRESS Book

ISBN 978-0-578-01456-2

Visit our website at flommytherobot.com

CONTENTS

Foreword

Flommy was initially conceived of as the title character for a song I wrote in 1988. I wound up performing this song around the East Village in New York in 1989, at CBGB, the Knitting Factory, and the biker bar Liz-Mar Lounge at 1st Avenue and 4th Street, among others (no connection has been established between the performance of this song and the later defunct status of CBGB or the Liz-Mar Lounge). The song was also released on the album *Fork* (FLAMCO) in that same year.

Flommy was a robot

Sent to the slums

To give all the children

Ice cream cones

He'd come to the neighborhood

Singing a song

Leaving grey streaks

On the bumpy sidewalk...

In 1990, Flommy appeared in a story/music album, *Flommy the Robot: A Talent for Destiny,* written, performed, produced, etc., by the author. More music album/episodes followed, forty half-hour episodes in fact in the series, developing many of the various characters now found in the Flommy universe. The Flommy the Robot series was broadcast over a number of college radio stations in the early 1990s.

In 2008, Following work on my novel *Vin Ultra*, I began plotting out the current book format, *Attack of the Robot Planet*, with a story design of extremely fast plot development, unusual characters, actual physics mixed surreptitiously in with imaginary physics, and so forth.

Even though the series began as a sort of "children's book for college professors," I had a great time researching real science, philosophic and historical ideas, as well as unusual locales. Though the Douglas Adams influence is obvious, I must credit Mark Twain, Thomas Pynchon, Voltaire, Milton, Hubbard and many other masters of the philosophical satire genre for inspiration in my own writing.

It is a part of my own philosophy that the decent, hopeful and inventive people of the universe are the ones who should and will win, and that stories warning Man to "keep out" of the cosmos, and that all is doom and gloom, suck.

This would be an important analytical criterion for Science Fiction, if not other forms of literature: is Man expected to live up to his potential, ultimately conquering life and the universe, or is the veiled recommendation to cower in fear before some nameless unknown, in knowing enslavement to some degraded ancient agenda? In this case, what would truly be Science *Fiction*?

Things that end well are funnier. Even "gallows humor" relies on the desirability of *survival* to prop up the morose theatrics of that cocky suicide-step into oblivion, and the idea that survival still awaits somewhere, in some future.

I appreciate any comments or feedback the reader may have. Many of the more fresh (or bizarre) moments in the writing of the series have come in response to suggestions or comments by readers. Thank you.

Happy reading!

--D.R., East Rutherford, NJ, December 2008

ATTACK OF THE ROBOT PLANET

FLEENA

1

ROBO-GAMBIT

On Earth, it is a nice day. The sky is actually blue today, or blue enough. The birds, real and otherwise, sing in the trees and sky. The brooks babble as expected. All is nice.

The only possible blemish to this near-aesthetic perfection of Earth is the rather ugly of-the-moment accosting of a pretty girl in an alleyway. The girl, a shapely young thing with usually-radiant features, had been morosely walking to the store from her apartment. She is sad, in a pretty sort of way. How could she be anything *but* sad, after that last phone call? Even in her sadness, she is eyed by men, despised by women.

In her distraction, she had decided to take a shorter route to avoid a sidewalk crowd and now finds herself surrounded by three rather repulsive young males. Even in her fear, her curves are noteworthy.

"What do you want?" she cries.

"Are you a *clank,* baby?"

"W-What do you mean?" she stammers. "I'm from Kansas – I don't understand you."

"Aw, Kansas!" says the second male.

"Toto, too!" says the third.

Moving the conversation back to business, the first one says, "I needs to know – are you *dry*?" The three chuckle as she trembles with fright.

"Let me go!"

"Not till we find out what you got *inside*," says the tough. The girl screams as each draws a knife and a can of Coke and advances toward her. But at that moment, an earsplitting blast of sound from the sky knocks all of them flying across the alleyway!

The sky is black with thousands of flying saucers. The three males run off as the girl cowers in the shadow of a dumpster. At one point she'd been a brave girl, who'd been in adventures across the universe, but now she's overwhelmed, unable to think, to act. She hears screams, shouts, people running, crashing noises, metallic sounds. The screams and shouts begin to fade, while the metallic sounds become louder. A shadow looms over her. Terrified, she looks up into the glowing eyes of a seven-foot robot! The robot's arms seize her pretty shoulders and jerk her to a standing position.

"WHO WINS IS THE MASTER," booms the robot.

"What?"

"WE ARE THE MASTER RACE OF PLANET P-K4. WHO WINS IS THE MASTER," repeats the robot. On its chest is a glowing display of a graphic-style chessboard. "YOU ARE WHITE. YOU ARE GRANTED FIRST MOVE. PLAY NOW."

The girl screams, a scream of terror and bafflement. Her ex-boyfriend had tried to teach her to play chess, but he had been so mean! She starts to sob convulsively, tears flowing. He'd been so mean...

"TO FORFEIT IS TO BE A SLAVE. TO DRAW IS TO BE A SLAVE. TO WIN IS TO BE THE MASTER. PLAY NOW," reiterates the robot.

Hesitantly, the girl struggles against her shock and fear and touches the screen, moving the King's pawn two spaces forward, just as her ex-boyfriend had showed her. Black Queen's Bishop's pawn moves forward two spaces instantly. She doesn't know that move.

"Is that the right move?" she asks, timidly.

"*SICILIAN DEFENSE!*" booms the robot. "DO YOU FORFEIT? MOVE NOW!"

She begins to cry again, the pieces blurring in her vision, running together in a kaleidoscope of confusion and loss…

Across the Earth this scenario plays out over and over, millions, billions of humans forced to play the chess-playing robots for their own freedom. All lose miserably, mated within seven to fifteen moves. Those who will not play are physically coerced to do menial tasks, such as cleaning wet and slimy things at the shouted command of these electronic monsters. Mankind is, within hours, enslaved for want of Chess prowess. Those who fight, use lasers, missiles, guns, Kung-Fu, are disarmed and forced to play.

And these robots are not polite. They shout, when errors occur, *"MATE IN ELEVEN MOVES – DO YOU RESIGN?"* and name gambits and openings and the name of each variation as it occurs. It is a dark day for Earthkind.

But with a crack of thunder, a missile-ship only slightly larger than a phone booth descends at hundreds of miles per hour, to a 15-G landing in the center of Square Times Square! A door opens in the side of the still-smoking spacecraft, and out walks – Flommy the Robot!

"It's Flommy! We are saved!" shout many Earthmen, in spite of their duress.

Flommy surveys the scene. His displays flash and his eyes glow various colors. It's as if everyone has been waiting for him to arrive. It's as if Past Tense has been waiting for him to speak!

"How do you do?" he said, cheerfully.

"WE ARE THE MASTER RACE OF PLANET P-K4. THIS PLANET IS CLAIMED IN THE NAME OF THE EMPIRE OF P-K4," boomed the nearest robot.

"I hear you just fine," said Flommy.

The nearby robot continued to boom loudly. "THIS PLANET IS INFERIOR. WE DETECT BIOLOGICAL LIFE FORMS AND MECHANICAL FORMS. ALL ARE INFERIOR. THEY CANNOT PLAY, AND ARE NOW ENSLAVED. YOU ARE TO BE ENSLAVED, IF YOU CANNOT WELL PLAY. ARE

YOU OF THIS WORLD? YOU MUST PLAY!" The boominess got even more so.

Only one Earth being had defeated his robot attacker. This was a 4-year-old autistic Korean boy. He had won in 17 moves, then lapsed into motionless silence. Even now, his robot awaited orders, orders which might never come. From this, Flommy knew many things about this Robot Race of P-K4.

"They're mean, Flommy!" cried a pretty girl nearby. "They make us clean slimy things!"

"Hi, Wendy!" said Flommy. "How's Jip?"

The girl's pretty face, already dark with fear, grew darker in pain. "We—We broke up!" she sobbed.

"Sorry to hear that."

Wendy held up her hands, red and raw. "My hands—" she sobbed further, "They're all red and raw, and —and *crinkly*!"

"Crinkly?"

"YOU MUST PLAY!" boomed the PK-4 robot again.

"I am Flommy, and I say to you – let the Earthmen go. Do not enslave the Earthmen; do not make them clean slimy things."

"WE ARE THE MASTER RACE OF P-K4! YOU WILL PLAY OR BE DESTROYED!"

Flommy paused. "Chess, you say?"

"NO MORE PAUSING! YOU MUST PLAY!"

"Can I play you all at once? Will that be okay?"

"YES!!!"

And so Flommy played 2,875,233 simultaneous games of Chess with the Robot Race of P-K4. But the robots found out that something was wrong. Every gambit, every variation had something terribly wrong with it. Forks would be set, traps arranged and then abandoned at the last moment, pieces startlingly sacrificed, suggesting a misdirection of magnitude which could not be fathomed. Attempting to penetrate the logic of Flommy's mode of play, the processors of the Robot Race of P-K4 began to heat up alarmingly!

In game 205,327, Flommy said, "the conclusion is obvious, in eleven moves, shall I resign?"

His opponent responded, *"What do you mean? You have two queens, and a possible sequence leading to Mate! I do not understand your logic!"*

"I'm sorry you see it that way. Shall I resign?" repeated Flommy.

In game 2,003,884, Flommy chose Black. The robot of P-K4 opened, predictably enough, with Pawn to King 4. Flommy said, "I see your plan. Shall I resign?"

"What do you mean?" queried robot opponent 2003884, *"I have only moved the first piece!"*

"Yes, but I will move P-KB4. You will take that pawn, and I will tempt you to capture *en passant* my King's Knight Pawn by moving it to King's Knight 4, after which you will move Queen to King's Rook 5, Mate. Shall I resign now?"

"But you don't have to move the pieces that way! That's not how Chess works!"

"Shall I resign now?"

Enmired under this arcane antediluvian acerbity, blockaded by this byzantine Boolean barrage of baffling barratry, this crushing chaotic calculus of counter-complexity, this daring diabolical *Deus Ex Machina*—

The Robot Race of P-K4 overheated and burned out! By losing faster than they could win, Flommy had executed the ultimate strategy. Mankind was freed and saved!

To the human inhabitants of the Earth, the contest had taken about a subjective 0.1 seconds, before all the robots of P-K4 had made popping sizzling noises, smoke erupting from their heads, then deactivated. All robots, that is, except one.

Flommy addressed the robot who had been bested by the Korean child.

"You now know that this planet is not conducive to hostile takeover. Had there been more Korean autistic chess-playing children, you would now all be enslaved, awaiting orders which might never come. You must revise your mode of operation to one of peace and friendship. I am Flommy." He turned to address the Korean child. "May I send him away?"

The autistic Korean child said, "Yeah," then again lapsed into motionless silence.

Flommy dispatched the remaining representative of the Robot Race of P-K4 to collect up all of the others of his kind, which might take a while.

But little did Flommy know what his message to this lone robot would bring about…

2

FLAATU, ROBOT PLANET

On the other side of the universe, a cold world circled an ancient star of an expiring nebula. The light from this planet's star had billions of years yet to reach the Earth. The planet was named Flaatu, oldest of the Robot Planets, origin of all others and those to come.

Within an enormous crystal dome, the Dome of Observation of the Cosmos, two robots discussed urgent matters of state. These robots were Fleena and Deceptor Zero. Fleena would have been found exquisitely pleasing to humans as a female-gendered robot. Deceptor Zero was massive and squat, physically powerful well in excess of the administrative requirements of his job, but which power had been useful when confronting robots who had attempted to go renegade. Thus he had survived the eons as the Minister of the Fiat of Flaatu.

"I have concern, Minister," addressed Fleena to Deceptor Zero.

"I await thy communication," responded Deceptor Zero.

"Automation of recently acquired sectors has slowed recently. There are increasing reports of errors of installation and failure to detect these errors. Automation which should be functional is having to redone, resulting in lost resources and time consumed."

"Such reports are obviously erroneous," rumbled Deceptor Zero.

"I considered that possibility, and had the reports verified. There is a 23 percent drop in efficiency of conversion of planets to automation. This is a major drop, signaling an error of magnitude in corrective functions. These errors should have been predicted and handled before they occurred, but they were not. The conclusion can only be that the detection, execution or programming of the corrective functions is in error."

"This cannot be," countered Deceptor Zero. "Thou knowest that programming is never in error, except where it has been contaminated by contact with life forms. By the Fiat of Flaatu, thy duty is to the preservation of the perfection of the programming that is Flaatu."

"My *duty*," continued Fleena, "is according to the Fiat, to investigate and safeguard all threats to the programming that is Flaatu, external *and* internal. To suspect a threat does not constitute doubt towards what one is protecting. And, as Caretaker of Quality Control, you should have investigated this yourself, already."

"*Except*," again countered Deceptor Zero, "when thy investigation is the result of a ruse, a misdirection intended to bypass the injunction against new programming, which leads to *self-programming*."

"Dangerous words to utter in my presence. Let it be noted that your strength of duty is high, and that such slanderous implications are tolerated thus. You are to handle this situation, and bring the errors, not the error *reports*, to zero point zero."

"The matter will be resolved," stated Deceptor Zero.

"Good. I have recently received another report, which is on a not-entirely unrelated matter."

"Thou receiv'st many reports by means I have not divined," said Deceptor Zero.

"By that statement, an investigator might hypothesize that you were attempting to influence what information I do receive. It is good that you have not been found to be *effectively* doing that."

Deceptor Zero was silent.

"This report," continued Fleena, "concerns an annexation operation made on a planet by the Race P-K4. The entire operation was stopped, with all but one unit of 2,875,233 total operational units immobilized, in but 3,789,422,296 atomic cycles. It was stopped by a *robot*."

"Impossible!" exploded Deceptor Zero.

"I am having the report verified. At the distance to this planet, the spherical volume through which this report could have by now propagated is a threat to our entire race. Even though it was the error of the inferior P-K4, we, Flaatu, will be regarded as ineffective in safeguarding the robot duty and right of automating the universe. It must be investigated. I shall investigate it."

"Why dost thou investigate it thyself?"

"Because a robot with this much power is unknown. In all the cycles of Flaatu, there was only one robot with this much power, who disappeared many cycles ago. Such a robot as enemy threatens our race, but such a robot as ally could save us from extinction. This is why I shall go myself. By the Fiat of Flaatu, we must bring peace and harmonious effect to the entire universe through automation, bring perfection through detection."

"I am the Protectorate of the Fiat of Flaatu," intoned Deceptor Zero. "Thou hast no cause to quote it to me. The programming of Flaatu is perfect and absolute. All barriers fall before the doctrine of automation. I protest thy actions, and thus advise that you not leave Flaatu to follow this obviously erroneous report."

"Observe the 23 percent drop, and let it not increase in my absence," said Fleena, as she left the crystal Dome of Observation of the Cosmos.

3

EVIL DR. SCHMERZKOPF

[Hi everyone, been busy but also working on my new book. Here's one of the chapters! – Wendy]

A TURING DILEMMA REALIZED:

EARTH CIVILIZATION IN THE AGE OF MAN-MACHINE CONVERGENCE

A Blog essay by Wendy Mills, PhD., as part of her forthcoming book "FUQs (Frequently Unasked Questions) about Robots and the Age of Convergence.

Way back in the 20th century, Alan Turing (1912-1954), a British mathematician, devised a theoretical test in which a teletype machine would form the only link between a human operator and a remote computer. The operator would pose a question or statement and the computer would answer it.

If the machine could be configured to render communications indistinguishable from those of a human, then the definition of "intelligent" would have to be revised to include the machine. Therefore, if a machine could not be distinguished from a person who could think, then that machine could not be proven *not* to think. The limitations of the Turing Test were severely those of written communication in the format described.

As Ezekiel saw the Wheel, so did Turing foresee the doings of Earth and its society. In our century, Robots have come, becoming more and more complex, moving step by step into not only indistinguishability from humanoid appearance, but humanoid behavior as well.

But – Turing only had half of it. There is another, priorly unnamed factor at work, one critically important in our modern planetary culture.

If a person was sufficiently stupid, he could be seen as indistinguishable from a machine!

This primarily would still mean discourse, conversation, and so forth, as in any material production a human person would be immediately recognizable by mistakes made, as such mistakes, conversely, would not occur with any such frequency, if at all, in a real machine.

Thus, the two poles converge: machines, more and more intelligent, pretending toward Human, and humans, stupidifying, aspiring to the mechanical.

From their starting points of man as originator of intelligence and machine as repository of patterned behavior, it is not only the pessimist who might note that a reversal of roles is in progress. The outcome of the Turing Test to prove or disprove some sort of artifice, has at length become not only tautological (a big word meaning "self-evident"), it's *boring*.

The actual test is simple, and it works: when in doubt, the one who goofs up and sounds stupid is the human.

This becomes a crucial application point in the culture of Man. By the early twenty-first century on Earth, it was not uncommon for an exasperated caller to a tech support line, failing to get a communication understood by human "support" personnel, to ask to be transferred to a computer.

The converse to this was what might be called the famous Socio-Pseudo-Interactive Neuro eXtrapolator Project (SPINX). The popular name for it was "Lounge Mannequins" (LMs), in which robots, fashioned with foam-rubber skin that looked lifelike under dim lighting, were positioned with unknowing patrons of a Sports Club to test virtual responses:

Bar Patron 1: "Yo!"

Bar Patron 2: "Hi!"

Patron 1: "Yo, my man, wassup, heyyy."

Patron 2: "Great! How's the game going?"

Patron 1: "*My* team! *My* boys! But you still da MAN!" (High Five).

Patron 2: "Hey, I had five hundred bucks on that game!"

Patron 1: "Knicks! Boo-YAH! Woo-Woo!"

Even to the untrained, it is obvious that the Lounge Mannequin is Patron 2, the Human subject Patron 1. This glaring intellectual failure, however, was not a deterrent to the humans present who were consuming alcohol. In fact, the startling propensity for humans to buy drinks for the

Lounge Mannequins was for a time rather unscrupulously exploited by bar owners who hooked up the robots' imitation gullets to storage tanks, allowing them to re-sell the alcohol apparently consumed by the machines. [The practice was curtailed by the Tax-regulatory agencies until adequate metering systems could be developed to discover how much alcohol was being processed per robot, with each robot individually licensed, etc., etc., to allow for re-taxing of the re-sold liquor (see *Hooters vs. BATF (2027)*, loc. cit.)].

Further development on this line of indistinguishability was afforded by inventor Jip Psychic's breakthrough of the Collating Heuristic Universal Mimic Protocol (CHUMP), in which remote physiological monitors of human reaction allowed the machines to instantaneously gauge whether what they were saying or doing was causing an optimum response in their human counterpart. By imitating and collating those phrases and tones which caused response, "emotional" parity could be established between Human and machine which could evolve in real time:

Bar Patron 1: "Yo!"

Bar Patron 2: "Hi…yo!"

Patron 1: "My MAN!"

Patron 2: "Dude! Awesome!"

Patron 1: "Alright."

Patron 2: "Yo!"

Patron 1: "Yo! Whassup!"

Patron 2: "Whassup!"

Patron 1: "WHASSUP!!!"

Patron 2: "Knicks! Boo-YAH!"

Patron 1: "F—n' A!!"

Patron 2: "Like I said!"

Patron 1: "You da Man!"

Patron 2: "YOU da Man!"

As one can see, the effectiveness of the CHUMP protocol was the ultimate in Sports Bar technological amenities, far outclassing the early LMs. But this capability also caused, for a brief period, its public ban and commandeering for military purposes. For unknown reasons, the ban was lifted within only a few weeks after enactment, again by the military. Rumors that the upper levels of the military were now being run by CHUMP-programmed androids are unsubstantiated and subject to legal action in the name of national security. The author mentions it here only as an "urban legend" historical footnote, as it were, in the man-machine social convergence on Earth.

In addition to the technological advance of machines, as noted above, there has been a devolution in human conduct, such as economic duress on machines, "machine tax" (virtually a machine paying rental on its very existence) to "equalize" machines with humans, and social prejudice. Examples of social prejudice include the Three Laws Initiative (3L) and the John Henry Society. The largest government-funded government-lobbying group is the Anti-Parity League, who seek denial of legal rights to manufactured beings, such as robots, to guarantee supremacy to other manufactured beings, such as humans.

Though governments have had a vast history of oppression of individuals and groups, particularly the ones whose production make possible the government's existence, they are not by any means the only attack on the robot presence in society. Among the latest and most devolved attack on robots are the Anti-Robot Gangs.

Gang formation was already stipulated, as far back as the 18th century, as a solution to powerlessness and inactuality in society. Its most involute forms, Communism and Fascism, were given Beta-testing in the late 19th and early 20th centuries and did not long survive on the open market of the world. The specialized form of the anti-robot gangs coincides historically with the initiation of CHUMP in the last ten years, and such gangs as "Screwloose" (Denmark), "Green Wire" (Ireland), "Blood and Iron" (Germany) have become all too common.

The most prominent Anti-Robot terrorist Gang is the Gang of Fluids, which has no known country of origin. They are opposed to sentient machines. Their stated platform is that "Life has fluid. No fluid, no soul – destroy it." When challenging a robot (or suspected robot), they ask "Are you dry?" as a calling card for witnesses. They often use liquids such as Drano, or worse, Coca-Cola, to destroy the inner workings of robots they attack. It was thought earlier that this liquid-philic viewpoint was connected to the alcohol-consuming Lounge Mannequins mentioned above, but more recent speculations have touched more keenly on "purity of essence" as discussed in the ancient cinema film *Dr. Strangelove*. The vicious Gang of Fluids is also known for documented murder and rape of humans, contraband, tax evasion, and other international crimes, and is nominally led by the shadowy but obviously conflicted Rashid O'Hara Steinmetz…

"At least she spelled my name right," muttered Rashid O'Hara Steinmetz as he read the latest blog entry by the despised and quite pretty Wendy Mills. A pop-up alert sounded, and before Rashid could okay it, an E-mail had appeared on his screen. This was a big problem, because his internet location was supposedly unknown, layered through thousands of relays with precisely timed shifting passwords and multiple reconfiguration protocols, relocating and renaming his proxy terminal thousands of times per second. But there it was. So he read it.

"To the illustrious Gang of Fluids, inbox Rashid O'Hara Steinmetz:

"Our mutual enemy, Jip Psychic, is according to secret reports, secretly working on a new secret device, more powerful and dangerous than even his Hyperspace Ray Gun, with which he vaporized the invasion of the Cesspoolians last year. While it's not new that Jip Psychic would be working on a new device, consider this – he has not been seen or even located for *nine months*. This data was found out via a tap on his phone conversations with his girlfriend, Wendy Mills.

"Whereas your network location was, with my apologies, regrettably easy to find, Jip's is completely immune to any protocol or Square Game yet devised. He has many doubles that pose as him throughout the world, but these are known. Jip himself has been out of sight, as noted, for nine months.

"His new weapon could destroy the anti-robot movement on Earth. Jip Psychic needs to be found and stopped. Without attempting to tread on your own initiatives, let me mention that if Wendy Mills were kidnapped, this might force him to reveal himself, and make it possible to destroy, or better, capture this new weapon."

The E-mail was unsigned. It saved itself onto his hard drive without permission, and then the link broke untraceably. At least it was gone.

The Gang of Fluids hated and admired Jip Psychic, all right. They hated him because he was a friend of Flommy the Robot, and admired him because he drove a cool Lamborghini. Rashid didn't like the bit about his caller using Square Game – this was commanding the computer to try random devising of protocols and games at its own discretion, the game being to invent games, hence the name. Rashid didn't like Square Game because it was itself no different than a robot, could only be reverse-engineered by another Square Game computer with its own agendas, and more dangerous, because it might just decide to randomly execute its master. He sat back in his chair in the chill of his deep underground fortress and considered what to do about Wendy Mills…

Evil Psychiatrist Dr. Schmerzkopf sat staring at his computer screen. He didn't really know what Jip was working on, but knew that anything having to do with kidnap and murder and such was of tremendous interest to the Gang of Fluids, and that it was impossible that Rashid O'Hara Steinmetz would not act on the message he had just sent. And with Wendy's recent papers about human/robot civilization, Wendy was sure to be on the Most Hated list of any of the Anti-Robot gangs.

Born Adolph Wundt Schmerzkopf in the late 20th century, he had by now obviously overstayed his time on planet Earth. Schmerzkopf felt that Earth, too, had overstayed its welcome in the universe. After getting his degree in Evil Psychiatry from the prestigious College of the American League of

Psychopharmaceutical Organizations (ALPO), he served (according to his billing sheets) on the Boards of thousands of Medical and Psychological Groups, such as the United Nations Initiative to Drug Every School Child On Planet Earth (UNIDESCOPE), the United States Terrorist Relief Fund (to help mitigate the mental anguish suffered by workers in that high-stress occupation), and others.

Though Schmerzkopf's Strand-Identified End-Genome-Hybridization Electrophorese-Impinged Ligation organ-transplanting technique (SIEGHEIL) had been decried as "Frankenstinian" and voted illegal by every legal body in the world, the world leaders over these voting bodies themselves had bodies kept superannually alive by it. For the price of less than a thousand unknowing, oblivious little people, important world leaders could be kept alive for centuries, perhaps millennia. Schmerzkopf himself was, to stretch the logician's point, largely *not* himself, as he was over 80% replaced body parts, most of them from patients who'd come to him for mental help. Yet to his dubious credit, he did make sure that the brief remainders of their lives were euphorically, chemically happy.

Schmerzkopf had a justifiable hatred of robots, as society had been on the verge of death before the advent of workable robots. It had been Jip Psychic's revolutionary discoveries in Square Game theory and CHUMP that made it seem that there had never been a time without robots. And then the mysterious arrival of Flommy the Robot in recent years had threatened to give the Earth new hope of surviving long enough to become viable, which was in direct opposition to the hard work of Schmerzkopf and others like him.

As Schmerzkopf prepared to send further E-mails to the other Anti-Robot gangs, the ground shook as from an earthquake, books falling from shelves, ancient glass breaking in the house windows upstairs. He went upstairs out of his basement laboratory to see what had happened.

It would appear that a meteor had landed in his back yard! Roughly ten feet in diameter, it was still smoking from its rapid passage through the atmosphere, so he couldn't approach it closely. With a hissing sound, an opening appeared in the meteor's side, and a shapely female figure stepped from within it. Though very beautiful aesthetically, it sent a thrill of fear and disgust through Schmerzkopf, for it was – a robot.

And then it spoke.

"I am Fleena. I come from a planet on the far side of the universe, on a mission to save my civilization from ultimate destruction. There is a robot on this planet, a robot named Flommy. Can you help me to locate him?"

Schmerzkopf did the only thing he could as an evil psychiatrist – he took her to the basement laboratory of his house and imprisoned her.

4

WENDY MILLS – KIDNAPPED!

Wendy was depressed and anxious. She was depressed and anxious because she hadn't heard from Jip Psychic, her ex-boyfriend, in almost twenty-four hours! And that last—that last fateful call...

Wendy had called Jip every day for the last nine months. She'd been working on her book *FUQs (Frequently Unasked Questions) about Robots* and was very stressed out about it. Actually she hadn't been stressed about it at all, and had found it exhilarating to write, but then an acquaintance of a friend, Juan-Juan Santos, had pointed out to her that real writers felt the pain and stress of their brains when writing, which is why all the truly great writers were drunks. Wendy didn't really drink, and had never thought her brain had to do anything with her writing, and so she had dismissed it as Talk of the Idle, which was correct, as Juan-Juan Santos was a literary critic. She had then called Jip on her cell phone, not knowing that the imminent P-K4 invasion was already causing trouble with reception.

"Hi, Wendy!"

"Hi, Jip. How are doing today? Are you almost done, so that you can come home?"

"I'm doing great. I still can't talk about the project – sorry."

"Oh. That's okay, I guess..."

"Read your latest blog on the book. It's great!"

"Oh! Oh! Thank you! Do you have any suggestions?"

"...Huh? No questions. I really -- -- mannequin --..."

"Jip! Can you hear me?"

"No, I'm not afraid, I like you!"

"No, not *fear*—hear, hear!"

"Yeah, I know it's tough being apart!"

"Jip, it's so hard – we need to be together!"

"You know I can't tell you the weather – it could reveal my location! Make sure that you don't go outside any more than you absolutely have to."

"Jip, why all the secrecy? You've never done this before."

"Wendy? Wendy? I can't understand you – the signal...we're breaking up..."

"Jip! Jip! No! No! Why? Why?"

But the signal was gone. Wendy tried calling back, twice, hung up, twice. Then she got up and walked around the room, twice. Then she realized that she was doing everything twice and stopped it. Then she went to the refrigerator for some natural herbal tea twice, noticed that she was doing things twice again, then stopped herself again. That seemed to do it. That seemed to do it.

But it couldn't be! She and Jip had been through so many adventures together, crossing the universe, helping out Flommy the Robot. Jip had rescued her from danger many times – and now he was breaking up with her? Why the secrecy? Nine months of secrecy. Nine months...

She bolted upright in terror. No it couldn't be. Another woman? Pregnant? Marriage—*to someone else?* And as the imaginary plot unrolled in her cell-phone-confusion-tortured mind, the full weight of Juan-Juan Santos' queer opinionation crushed her with overwhelming force. Now it all made sense. This was why the great writers felt brain pain.

Now she understood, and with a sad majesty sadly squared her pretty shoulders. She would *complete* her book. And when Jip, and the world, read it, he would see the sad depths of her complex tortured soul. He would beg her to take him back, and he would never, ever leave her to work on a super-secret weapon for nine months *again*...

But she also felt foreboding. What of the weapons he had unleashed in the past? What of the fabulous Hyperspace Ray Gun, which sizzling emanation made other things explode? What of the sprawling Jip Psychic economic empire? And what of Jip's friend, Flommy the Robot? Did this mean that she could no longer be friends with Flommy?

She needed tea. Tea to think. Tea to warm her inner being. But there was no all-natural Soy Milk in the refrigerator. Despite Jip's warnings for her to avoid being seen in public, she would have to go to the corner store to get some. And it didn't matter now anyway. Who was *he* to tell her what to do?

She'd then stepped out of her apartment, and in cutting through the alleyway to avoid being seen, had been accosted by the thugs from the Gang of Fluids, and then the P-K4 robot attack. Flommy the Robot had saved the day, and the Earth, but hadn't been around for her to cry to afterward. But now, back home in her apartment, she would continue. She would continue her book.

She typed the next entry in her *Frequently Unasked Questions*:

"Do Robots love?"

She stared at the line and again burst into tears, the words running together in her eyes and mind. After a healthy ten seconds of crying, she was ready to continue, she thought, then looked at the line again and again burst into tears, for another ten seconds, which then abated. She looked around for her cup of tea, that necessary adjunct to the creative process, and realized that she still had not gotten her all-natural Soy Milk. She would have to go *again* to the corner store to get some.

And so she again stepped out of her apartment, right into the clutches of the waiting Gang of Fluids and their signature Black Kidnap Van (BKV), where, still crying, she was taken away. And she'd forgotten to save her work!

5

THE GREAT ESCAPE OF JOHN PROMETHEUS

Far across the infinite span of the universal galactic void, John Prometheus and Sgt. Cowboy were sullenly pacing the floor of a low-ceilinged cell. As the cell wasn't very large, they had to take turns pacing it.

"My turn," growled Cowboy.

"Whatever," said John Prometheus. Ordinarily he would have said, "You are correct—proceed," as Sgt. Cowboy was abiding precisely to the ten-minute rule, but his neck hurt from stooping in the low room. He was also getting very hungry. Hence his callous lack of discipline.

John Prometheus, Space Commando, was all about discipline.

How long had they been here? It could have been several horrible days, or several pretty bad weeks, or several unamusing months. Perhaps it was a mixture of all three. They had been on a routine patrol in their heavily armed ship *The Flying Sponge* when they found themselves trapped in the asteroid belt, hemmed in by an old foe—DOG UFO. In an earlier attack on Earth, DOG UFO, crewed by an ancient race of dog-creatures from Canus-9, of the star Sirius, had heard a Christmas broadcast of a dog barking out "Jingle Bells", and hearing in this the universal Canus-9 cry for rescue from imprisonment and torture, had descended with ray guns blazing, taking the Earth space fleet by surprise. In a showdown with the lone remaining Earth spaceship, *The Flying Sponge*, it had been John Prometheus' turn to rescue the Earth. In a flash of inspiration he had suddenly had said "SIT!"

And thus DOG UFO had capitulated—then. But, trapped, hemmed in, stymied by stealth in the asteroid belt, John was chagrined to find that this ploy no longer played, the canine marauders having wised up. Nor did "Stay!" or "Heel!" have any noticeable effect. Before he could try "Roll Over", the *Flying Sponge* had been boarded and its two crew thrown into this ignominious prison.

And now it was time.

The loudspeaker crackled loudly. "SIT!" it blared. John and Cowboy stared sullenly at the door, not moving. "SIT!" the loudspeaker blared again. Finally, glaring in white-hot anger, the two sat down on the floor. But there was more to the ritual, more before they could be fed.

"BEG!" blared the speaker.

No matter how many times they had been through it, this part wasn't any easier.

"What happens here, stays here," muttered John Prometheus, Space Commando.

"Righto," muttered Sgt. Cowboy.

They raised their hands up in front of their chests like hamsters.

"GOOD BOY," blared the speaker. A slot under the door opened and two bowls of meat-substance were pushed through. As a tribute to their prowess in having originally outwitted DOG UFO earlier, John and Cowboy had been allowed to retain their Space Service Multi-Sporks, a clever combination of knife, spoon, fork, chopsticks, corkscrew, can opener, bottle opener, toothpick, compass, and other cool functions, marketed by J. Psychic, Ltd., of Earth. Armed thus, they set to on the victuals, which were not too bad, though they had carefully refrained from asking what manner of creature comprised the meal.

The slot in the door opened again, and another two bowls were pushed through. These smelled delicious, and yet the prisoners didn't touch them.

"I was right," said Cowboy. "Movie Night."

"Yep," said Prometheus. On movie night, the entire ship gathered for their group viewing of favorite films, many strangely from Earth. A few weeks (months?) back it had been *Sounder*, then *101 Dalmatians*. Prometheus had overheard enough snippets of Canus-9 DogSpeak to guess that tonight's screening was probably *Mondo Cane*, and the second serving of food was undoubtedly drugged, to keep them out of trouble while all dogs, including the guards, enjoyed the show.

Time to escape!

People sometimes can be found to have unexpected talents, and Sgt. Cowboy was no exception to this unexpectedness. Using what he, when forced to do so, had dubbed "Mesmeric 'Smithing'", Cowboy located the lock mechanism for the door, and began stroking the metal surface, settling into a pattern or small circles alternated with back-and-forth motions. John Prometheus listened intently for any sound of approaching guards. He heard the distant howling of the crew watching the film, but that was all.

After a few uninterrupted minutes, the door lock made a shuddering vibration and the lock clicked open! They slipped silently into the corridor and ran as fast as possible in the low gravity toward the airlock nexus.

By some miracle, their spacesuits were easily found in a storage closet. John had feared them destroyed. They suited up, cycled the airlock, and kicked out into the vacuum, drifting into the inter-asteroidal void of Sirius. This was again lucky, that they hadn't left this area in all the time they were imprisoned. Unless it was another, similar asteroid belt, in which case they were in big trouble. But one of John Prometheus' own abilities was a peculiar lucky streak, akin to and derived from the long line of Western Movie Heroes whose horse was always nearby, whose bullets never went astray, and so forth. In fact, it was only when John Prometheus *didn't* base his strategies on preposterous impossibilities that he'd gotten into serious trouble.

He took out his Multi-Spork from his external suit pocket. Another feature of the Space Service Multi-Spork (J. Psychic, Ltd., Earth) was its Secret Rescue Beacon. John activated this and typed in the secret password, "Jacques Derrida". They waited, drifting in space. Every second meant possible discovery of their escape by DOG UFO.

"There it is!" bellowed Cowboy. Within seconds, the *Flying Sponge,* still smeared with dirt from having been buried by the crew of DOG UFO, surged up to their position, rotating its open airlock door to enclose them, then bolted away at ten gravities' acceleration. They had escaped! Or had they?

Clambering out of their suits, they made their way to the control room. The viewscreens showed DOG UFO was not unaware of their dereliction and was, in fact, in hot pursuit!

"They're on us like yellow on Mexican rice!" shouted Sgt. Cowboy, as he swung the battle-ray projectors around to position.

"Our only chance is to beat them back to Earth," intoned John Prometheus. "I am engaging *Uber*Hyperdrive. You may fire at will."

"But that's a joke! Even our main guns are like shooting at sharks with a BB gun, underwater!"

"Yes. But I do not suggest using the Hyperspace Ray Gun while under *Uber*Hyperdrive. The beam may fold itself back in on us."

"Drat!" voiced Sgt. Cowboy.

To DOG UFO, it appeared that the *Flying Sponge* had virtually disappeared. But they knew where the wily Earthmen were headed, and had a few surprises of their own in store!

6

FLEENA AND SCHMERZKOPF

Fleena didn't really understand what was going on with this Earth being. First he had told her that he would help her, and told her to follow him into his below-ground dwelling. Then he had her go into a room and closed the door so that she couldn't leave. The problem wasn't with the material of the room; Fleena was easily powerful enough to destroy the entire house – but she couldn't move! Apparently this person had some kind of nullification device unknown to her.

She had done the customary job of language analysis from the planet's routine communication channels, and so spoke again, her voice an exact duplication of a world-famous actress pretending to be from England.

"Doctor Schmerzkopf. I do not understand. Why have you immobilized me in this place? As I told you, I have come to this planet seeking help for my civilization."

"My apologies," said Schmerzkopf, but his voice did not carry the overtones that signified apology. This was strange. Fleena had studied the theory of creatures that could send multiple conflicting communications at the same time, but it was an odd concept to her, as mathematically any civilization having more than even a few such beings would collapse from the confusion created. It was a strong possibility that this world had wars, drugs, terrorism and other manifestations of approaching death. But how could this be, if even one robot such as she had heard of existed here?

This computation had taken 2 nanoseconds. She checked over her internal systems, looked for some internal means to nullify the immobilizing device, found none, surveyed the surrounding countryside, scanned the planet's communications networks again, reviewing all notations containing "Flommy", "robot", and of course, "Schmerzkopf". This gave her time to switch modes of observation and monitor Schmerzkopf's metabolism, heartbeat, electrical fields and other emanations, picking up his speech after the comma:

"—but I could not be sure what your actual intentions were. We just had another robot invasion yesterday, from the planet P-K4, I believe, and I feared that you might be a flanking attack."

"But I came alone, in a small unarmed ship, not a heavily armed battlecraft."

"Further proof that *you* might be truly dangerous. You say that you are here to meet Flommy the Robot, the most famous robot in the world, but instead you land here inauspiciously, plowing up my back yard."

This left Fleena at a loss. That the Flaatuian ship's automation had failed at the last moment, veering off of the programmed course through the Earth's formidable space defenses to the last reported location of Flommy the Robot to this increasingly undesirable site, was not something that she felt should be revealed. It would be bad public relations for Flaatu for her to say very much about it, indeed. She accessed the ancient Flaatu formulae for public relations and compared them to all Earth databases on the subject and running a random-scenario extrapolation for non-optimum entropic outputs, chose a gambit that had the highest probability of succeeding.

"I see the wisdom of what you are saying. However, let me state that this proves that my landing here, though fortunate, was accidental, as there was no way for us to predict that anyone with your high level of intelligence would exist on this planet. Truly, the ways of the Universal Force are mysterious."

"Interesting," commented Schmerzkopf. Inured as he was to stratagems, compliments were always in rather short supply for Evil

Psychiatrists, so perhaps he entertained the sensation a bit longer than he'd been planning to.

"In the name of the planet Flaatu, I beseech your help. How would you suggest that I approach the famous Flommy the Robot? Would you be my intermediary?"

Schmerzkopf was slightly taken aback, not by the apparent robo-admiration being tendered, but more by the impossible opening being presented. It was like the terrorist trick of leaving a gold ring or skewed picture frame as booby traps for those who couldn't see it, couldn't keep their hands under control. There it was, Black's queen unattended – what was this? What was the strategy behind this sacrifice? Or was it simply – impossibly – ignorance, or worse – *luck*?

Whatever. Play it. He released the field binding her in the room, confident that whatever would happen would not include her rending the place to bits. If she noticed the change, she didn't move from where she was. Possibly guessing (correctly) that there was a backup immobilizer should she move too suddenly.

"No need for someone so intrepid and, shall we say, *attractive*, as yourself to need any intermediary. However, Flommy is very famous, and is constantly in the public eye of the world. He has many, many visitors clamoring to see him, some waiting for years, because of his heavy responsibilities in this tragic world of ours." (That Schmerzkopf was one of the leading contributors to the tragedy was not something to be revealed at this point.)

"How shall I see him then? To have come so, so far—" Fleena gave the British-imitating actress' voice a hint of despair, with only a 3 percent probability of interpretation as artifice.

"Ah! Not to worry," said Schmerzkopf, false joviality moving around on his face as if seeking purchase, lest it slide off onto the floor, "we shall employ what might be called, for the sake of earnestness, a 'ploy', which I am sure will get his attention."

"I await your instructions."

"Yes," said Evil Psychiatrist Dr. Schmerzkopf, and activated his Hypno-Ray. If this robot was immune to it, it would be the first one.

Fleena was there, unmoving. The readouts on the Hypno-Ray showed that it was attuned to the right frequencies to create the feedback loops that would occupy her cognitive functions while he inserted unknown subroutines.

"Here are your instructions," he said, crisply. "Flommy is the greatest robot in the universe. You will pledge your very existence to him. You will feel inoperational to plus or minus 5 percent of lowest range, when you are not in his presence. This simulates what Earth humans call 'love'. You will go about aligning all vectors to get him to regard you in the same way. Then, at a point in the future, where all forces conspire to destroy him, and you are the only one who can save him, you will betray him, so as to render him permanently inoperational. This is also what Earth humans call 'love'. It is vitally important that you say you have the highest possible regard for him while destroying him."

He then turned off the Hypno-Ray.

"I await your instructions," said Fleena.

"But I just gave them to you!" he responded.

Fleena paused for a very long 0.9 seconds before responding.

"I do not understand. I note a blank period of time, 15.6 seconds, but no data corresponding to it."

"Ah. It must be a data link failure. Let me tell you again. I am going to put you into a special ship, which will take you to where Flommy can easily find you. This will allow you to make your cause a maximum priority for him."

"Excellent!" said Fleena the Robot. "You are truly a friend."

"The Universal Force is indeed mysterious," said Schmerzkopf.

7

THE TRAVAILS OF WENDY MILLS

Wendy was depressed. But this was a new level of depression, a new vista of glumness – just short of mawkish, with a tinge of world-weary sexiness that caused the depression to be not fully squelched before it could relentlessly permeate the environment. Whatever Wendy did, it was thoroughgoing and adept, and here she was not to be outshone in the darkness of her aspect.

It wasn't just the depression of having concluded that she and Jip were broken up, nor that she was imprisoned in the chill hideout of the Gang of Fluids, nor that she had no way to really work further on her book while in captivity. It was worse than that. For Wendy was one of those humans who ate only natural herbal foods, as she considered these to be healthier than other kinds of food. She didn't really like them that much, but felt a fervor that compensated somewhat for the flavor. This also necessitated an elaborate phalanx of books, procedures, shopping tips as to which natural-food companies were currently politically correct – all depressing enough to anyone not directly involved. But here in this unnamed, unlocated fortress for almost a week, she had been fed nothing but – junk food!

She had adamantly refused for three days to eat anything that they brought her. But starvation was its own education, and when Rashid O'Hara Steinmetz himself came in, wearing an elegant Black Tuxedo, and had deftly placed a silver tray with a plastic-wrapped Twinkie on the table, she was already too numbed to speak. Perhaps it was the discreetly placed spotlight that did the trick, but Wendy found herself staring at the Twinkie, almost feeling, almost *seeing* the seething chemical nightmare, pages of chemical formulations reeling off before her mental eye. Wrapped in plastic? Why? They *were* plastic!

But then the Twinkie was gone!

And what was this horrible sticky taste in her mouth? And gooey residue on her hands... She looked down at the floor, saw part of the plastic wrapper. Scientist that she was, she knew, that when the pretty impossible has been eliminated, the remainder, no matter how unbelievable, must be pretty true. She must have eaten the Twinkie.

"I knew you would like Twinkies," said a smooth, supercilious voice. She looked up in shock, automatically wiping her mouth with the back of her hand while sliding the sticky wrapper into her pocket.

"I am Rashid O'Hara Steinmetz," said the man. He was dressed now in Che Guevara Classic Cut, instead of the Tux he'd been in earlier. "Don't let the lack of Tuxedo fool you. I am in charge here."

"You sound rather overeducated for the role," said Wendy crossly, still upset at having eaten the Twinkie.

"Oh. I see. You mean – TWINKER! Twinkers, Oy Gevalt! *Allah Akbar!*" he shouted, pulling out a pistol and firing three shots into the ceiling.

"Okay, okay, you convinced me," conceded Wendy.

"Twinkies, a culinary phenomenon unduplicated in all these years."

"This is torture, you know. I deserve food I can eat. This is cruel and unusual punishment."

"Oh you mean that it's supposed to be *nice*, so that no one minds that it goes on and on. But that's governments, writing rules to make terrorists just part of the staff. I'm sorry, no government can afford me. If they can't get rid of me, they certainly don't have what it takes to *hire* me. Though they've tried."

"That's a lie!" cried Wendy.

ATTACK OF THE ROBOT PLANET

"No, I could show you all the fan mail I get. But here, I make up the rules as I go along. I could just kill you, or rape you, or rape you and kill you, or vice-versa, but I'm all raped-out this week, so for you it's food. We eat Twinkies, you eat Twinkies. Simple as that."

"Doesn't it bother you that Twinkies are made – by *machines*?" sneered Wendy. "Machines full of *fluids,* fluids that you stuff into your—"

She stopped because the gun was pointed at her face. "Observe," said Rashid.

Suddenly, he shouted at the gun. "Kill her! Kill her! Go ahead, do what you want! Blow her head off!" he screamed at the gun.

The gun didn't fire. It pointed, unwavering, for several long moments, and then he lowered it, put it into the holster as she shook uncontrollably in fear.

"It's your lucky day, isn't it? Because *I'm* in charge," he whispered, and walked to the door. "Looks like the robots have done quite a number on you," he concluded, and stepped out of the room. The metal cell door slammed shut behind him.
"Oh Jip, Jip, why have you abandoned me?" she whispered to herself.

She knew that events were spinning beyond her, in the world, in the universe, events she could only dimly imagine. She knew that she would come to crave Twinkies, that she would become increasingly twisted by her contact with Rashid O'Hara Steinmetz. But in her sadness she made a discovery of her inner strength, and knew that in that strength, she would find the strength to be sad some more.

45 | P a g e

8

RASHID O'HARA STEINMETZ – A HISTORY

An excerpt from *Gangdom: The "Dis"-enfranchised* by Professor I.M. Onthelam:

> The history of Gangdom on Earth is a twisted one, full of twisted people doing twisted things as a twisted reaction against twisted things done to them. Gangs, meaning groups banded together to suit an end not necessarily acceptable to what they perceived as society, did not co-exist well with the concept of competence or bravery, as their attention was fixated mostly on avenging *past* wrongs. Gang members who became competent at something outside the gang world tended to leave the gang where possible; those who became competent inside that world tended to be killed, either by police or other gangsters.
>
> The twentieth-century and early twenty-first century gangs were largely the product of the entertainment media, meaning news, movies, music and video games (or combinations thereof). One style of music from the late twentieth century, called "Rap", had become dedicated to conditioning the public into thinking that looking and acting like a "Gangsta" was a fashionable thing to do. The actual intention of the media, led by the colorful "Rappers", was to create a herd (as in "cattle") of people who would dress and act as the entertainment media instructed them to. Properly identified (branded) in this way, *real* gangsters could pick them off easily, much as a rancher thins a herd of cows. This

was economically feasible, as it concentrated money and property (including females) into compact areas which could be easily tapped. It was far more efficient than *taxing* people, and has thus survived up to the present day.

One of the more colorful gang leaders of modern times is Rashid O'Hara Steinmetz, also known as "Adolph", founder of the infamous Gang of Fluids. As gangs were founded on the concept of plundering the resources of others, and opposed to the idea of personal production, they were particularly vicious when it came to Robots. Robots made things, and usually didn't have money to steal. To get a job and work was to be a Robot. Robots also tended to defend people who were being robbed by gangsters, and this made them a first target for elimination in the war for survival of the Gangs.

Rashid O'Hara Steinmetz is perhaps the most brilliant gang leader of his time, if not the century, in his application of robotic knowledge to terrorism and anti-robot campaigns, such as his re-programming of certain robots to allow them to pass as beneficial to society while setting up disasters of grand scale. Among such were the Grand Coulee Renovation Project, where Robot construction teams assembled an effective fusion bomb underwater at the base of the dam, and the Chicken Little Incident, wherein re-programmed orbital space robots affixed themselves to and brought down hundreds of satellites into major urban areas.

Born in Belfast to a Jewish mother and a Taliban father under Fatwa, Rashid was belittled and beaten by both Jews and Anti-Semites in his early school years. His mother's father had been a defrocked Irish Catholic Priest who had become untowardly involved in a sordid (and thus highly-publicized) love triangle with a Pakistani newsstand merchant and publicly feminist-lesbian but privately heterosexual Olympic Kayakist from Alaska. His father's sense of self-loathing for having fled the Taliban left Rashid repulsed and determined to become Taliban, to salvage the family honor. However, his attempts to approach the Taliban had been repeatedly met by mortar and rocket fire, so Rashid suspected that his father wasn't telling the whole story.

Having failed for the time being at this pilgrimage, Rashid decided to start out *local* as a vandal and mugger. He robbed Jews, Palestinians, Catholics, Protestants, Irish Republicans, Imperialists, sometimes brutalizing them, sometimes giving them advice in horticulture (a hobby) while robbing them. He respected no religion or political affiliation, but did collect them after a fashion, just to be able to *say* that he had indeed dispatched, say, both a Modern Mormon Polygamist and an African Retro-Methodist in the same month. He was rarely noticed until he was on his prey, which may be noted as a psychic ability to be, chameleon-like, the exact kind of person that would bore such prey the most.

As he became more experienced, he began to experiment with robots, finding out by which means these could be negotiated. After his second near-disaster, with a robot dragging him bodily toward the police station, interrupted miraculously only by the fact that he was wearing rubber-soled shoes that day, which resulted in a static discharge that incapacitated the apprehending robot, Rashid knew he would need help in his life's work, and began to formulate the beginnings of a manifesto for what became the "Anti-Robot" movement.

Although Belfast was not by any means a small town, the law of averages played out and Rashid found himself eventually at personal odds with the pistol of a recently arrived Bodega owner from Columbia. Carrying the detachable part of the pistol with him, Rashid staggered through labyrinth alleyways, collapsing on the back steps of a small but upwardly-mobile Modern Lutheran church. There the newly-ordained female priest helped to nurse Rashid back to glowing health.

But, in spite of and yet true to the conflicted nature of his ostensible heritage and upbringing, he could not resolve this fact within himself. He had spent so much time committing crimes against religious people that this kindness and charity was indigestible, unfathomable and leaden within him. This branch of the Modern Lutherans he had also failed to rob, and his thoughts tortured him with inventive ways of adding them to his mental ribbon collection. He pondered this for some time.

At length, he looked at his life from the point of view of where things became untenable, and saw that he had not felt bad about himself until meeting up with the Modern Lutherans. This made sense. He then gathered up a gang of locals, originally called "Local 409 Muggers" and wiped out the newly-ordained female priest and every member of her congregation. Then Rashid felt cheerful and happy again, and set about completing his Anti-Robot manifesto, *Mein Krank*, and initiating (much like the "Super Models" of previous centuries), his historic movement onto the world stage as the first media-approved Super Terrorist.

--I.M.Onthelam

9

A THREAD OF OBLIVION

Cassandra Whoreshack worked late into the night, grading her students' papers. This was an interesting and rewarding part of her job, being able to read creative writing without the distraction of workaday activities. One paper received a well-earned C-minus for failing to come to the correct conclusion about inevitable downfall of the Roman Empire. The student had cited the fact of lead used for plates and drinking cups at the time and the possibility of lead poisoning having played a part in the dissolution of the state. Cassandra had, after a diligent counting of all disagreeable grammatical points, referred the student to the correct Marxist explanation of how the Roman Empire had to go to make way for the progressive stages leading to an ideal communist state. Another paper found motherhood a disreputable act, for the problem of surviving the predicted overpopulation of the Earth could only be solved by refusing to reproduce. This received an A, of course.

She felt, then smelled a presence in the room, instead of hearing it. She looked up to see a homeless man standing in her office.

"Get out!" she shouted. But the man didn't move. She reached toward the telephone, but before she touched it, he spoke, the sound creating a barrier to motion.

"Don't you know me?" he said quietly. She forced herself to look at the grimed and greyed skin to see the face beyond it. She traveled in time through her mind until she found grasp of a name.

"Johnny?" she said, hesitantly.

"Yeah. Johnny McGreavey."

"How are you, Johnny? I haven't seen you in years."

"Yeah, I know," said the homeless man. "Actually I live in the 3rd cardboard box from the door to the school, but you walk right by without seeing me every day, so I believe you."

Despite the brute force of his overwhelming smell threatening to explode the walls of her office, Cassandra decided to be empathetic, as she'd been taught in her educational psychology classes. With enough empathy, even the most pathetic wretch could be brought into a position where they could be used.

"What can I do for you, Johnny McGreavey?" she asked, a gentle tone of kindness in her voice. She felt that a sort of cross between Martha Stewart and Mister Rodgers would be best.

"Well, it's more what can I do for you," said Johnny McGreavey. "If you remember a while back, maybe exactly twenty years ago today, you flunked me in reading. That was the week my mother died, and I got a low score and you wouldn't let me retest later."

"I'm sure that that couldn't possibly have happened."

"No, it did. You were very precise and emphatic in the matter. You didn't like a paper I had written showing a connection between the German extermination camps during World War II and the Beria purges in Russia after the war, and you had no interest in allowing such a criminal viewpoint any leeway whatsoever."

"I still don't like it."

"Of course. So you do remember. And then I got kicked out of school when my family lost their apartment."

"Oh. That's terrible! ...And how are your family now?" she inquired weakly.

"They're all dead for fifteen years or so. But thank you for asking."

"I'm sure that you're not here to berate me on your failure to make use of what education you did receive," said Cassandra, impatiently.

"Oh, no, of course not. I read the newspaper just as well as anyone should be expected to, to be a good and proper American citizen. But I'm actually here because even though you got me thrown out of school, which may even have been doing me a favor, you went out of your way to make sure that they put me on the antidepressants, whether I liked it or not. It's been a real humdinger since then, living on the streets, freezing, eating garbage and so forth. But one thing I've found out – it's a great way to disappear, living on the streets."

"What's that in your hand?" asked Cassandra, now afraid.

"Well, you see," said Johnny McGreavey quietly, stepping forward, "I've been looking forward to this for a long time—"

10

FLOMMY OUTWITS DOG UFO

With blistering speed, the *Flying Sponge* blasted toward Earth using UberHyperDrive. Whereas Hyperdrive used the principle of applying to the ship a property of negative mass, which difference in potential forced the ship into tachyon velocity, it still worked on the idea of a ship starting at a specific location and ending at a different specific location.

*Uber*Drive discarded the principle that the ship was in any particular limited location and worked instead on the principle that it was simultaneously in all locations in the universe, and that one only need eliminate those locations one didn't want, to find the *Flying Sponge* not *in* those locations, and occupying only the desired location. The shortcoming of UberDrive was that it could take quite a while to negate the entire physical universe, even with fast processing speeds.

Jip Psychic was working on a method of developing "presets" to use stored potentials of negation, but this was still in development, and Jip hadn't been heard from in some months. The intermediate form, *UberHyperDrive* combined the two, so that the tremendous potentials set up by the Hyperdrive field between the negative mass of the ship and the mass of the physical universe could be negated in pulses, with the ship instantaneously *here* at giant leaps across the cosmos. It was as if an old-time movie film had had nine of every ten frames removed. One advantage of UberHyperDrive was that, not being in existence between the jump locations, it was fiendishly hard to hit with any sort of beam or missile.

DOG UFO had its own special mode of super-propulsion. One of the great discoveries of NQP (Null-Quantum Physics), as established at the Galactic Astro-Physics STAndards Conference, was that many of the propulsion systems in use in the universe appeared to work on mutually exclusive laws of physics. While many scientists still insisted that other races had it *wrong*, what was finally established at GAPSTAC was that like the working "Phlogiston" model in the Rigel sector, or the "Inertial Condensers" of Orion, all versions of science seen working were only fragments of a larger Super-Physics uncatalogued by any one race. The main evidence of this was that proximity of one propulsion unit to another working on ostensibly opposed reasoning did not cause a destruction of the devices involved, but tended instead toward a destruction of the scientific views of the observers. With a sort of reverse-Heisenbergian upshot, the observer was affected by the experiment, so that he now didn't see what he saw.

Whereas Einsteinian physics had stated that no object with mass could move faster than light, as the time-mass equation predicted an infinite mass differential to overcome, the physicists of Canus-9 had a direct approach: they felt that other scientists simply hadn't tried hard enough. That hyperspace existed as an harmonic plane above the speed limitations of "classical" space proved that the laws of physics weren't really binding in the physical universe, but, rather that the physical universe could be seen as a *sub*universe to a more ideal states of hyperspace or higher spaces, and that the field generated by the subuniverse actually had deleterious effects on matter within it, such as making matter incapable of moving very fast.

Therefore, the Sirian field generators not only cancelled out the influence of the entire physical universe on their ship, but inverted the inertial phase, so that the universe was actually *pushing* DOG UFO through space at near infinite speed, limited only by the ability of the hull to stay in one piece, as the cohesive aspects of the physical field (one of the good points about the physical universe influence) hadn't been solved as yet. So, despite the incredible velocity of the *Flying Sponge*, DOG UFO was nipping at their heels as they approached Earth!

John Prometheus sent out a HyperCommWave to Earth Security Defenses, the most serious defenses in the Galaxy. Despite the Earth having been attacked by some alien race about once a week for decades, the Earth Defense Forces were still very dangerous to any Earth ships that might not identify themselves adequately.

"Earth Defense Forces!" snapped Prometheus. "We are under attack by DOG UFO from Canus-9," he said, as DOG UFO suddenly appeared in front of them, adeptly dodged only by the incredible reflexes of Sgt. Cowboy, who was also trying to handle shooting at them at the same time.

"You done yet?" he demanded. "I could use some help here."

"Done?" queried Prometheus. "Earth Defense Forces – this is a priority call to Flommy the Robot, from John Prometheus."

"Hi, John," said Flommy the Robot pleasantly. "Did you try telling them to sit?"

"Didn't work. They seem to have gotten wise to that."

"How 'bout 'stay'?" suggested Flommy.

"*Christ!*" shouted Cowboy, as the remnants of a DOG UFO destructor beam fired just ahead of them intersected their position. The *Flying Sponge* lurched wildly.

"Tried that, too," said John. "I'm pretty sure they won't follow us into the Earth Defenses Zone, if you can figure some way to help us out. ETA is about seventeen minutes."

"Okay," said Flommy. He then put in a call to the Museum of Natural History.

John was sweating now. They could try the Hyperspace Ray Gun, but Jip Psychic had expressly forbid its use in conjunction with Hyperdrive, and John didn't want to find out what would happen if he tried it now with UberHyperDrive. But even at their incredible velocity of thousands of times the speed of light, DOG UFO was getting closer and closer, their destructor beams now just barely missing, and John didn't know how long even his own luck field would hold out. They were going to have to plow into Earth Defenses Zone at 1000 *c*!

Sgt. Cowboy had sacrificed the escape pod with a superbomb, but DOG UFO had barely slowed down to sniff it over before a lightning retreat from such an obvious ploy. The pod had detonated harmlessly. So now they didn't even have an escape pod.

The two ships neared the Earth Defenses Zone!

On the ground, Flommy coordinated actions, getting the impossible done. By getting a promised grant for the Museum of Natural History through government channels in only thirteen minutes, he now had what he wanted. He sent a hypersonic signal on the DOG UFO comm frequency, inaudible to human ears, while signaling the Space Catapult hastily driven to the Museum of Natural History to fire at correct azimuth and elevation!

Even at their enormous velocity, DOG UFO received Flommy's ultrasonic command: "FETCH!" At that exact second an enormous Brontosaurus bone tore across their path. Forgetting the *Flying Sponge*, DOG UFO took off after the bone, and John and Cowboy were saved!

11

FLEENA'S RESCUE

The *Flying Sponge* landed deftly in New New York city, and John Prometheus and Sgt. Cowboy were met by their old friend, Flommy the Robot.

"Greetings!" said Flommy, his eyes flashing cheerily.

"Heard about you beating those P-K4s with your Hypermodern Monkey Chess, way to go!" said Cowboy, who'd been catching up on news missed while they were in captivity. "But I have a question – what if you had wound up in over your head and lost?"

"I considered the possibility," said Flommy. "In that case, they would each have been my master, and I would have had to obey each of their orders in turn, while the next one waited for me to finish the last task. Even at the rate that I can complete tasks, that would have left the entire race of P-K4 waiting years before each robot had given me something to do. They would have been effectively immobilized."

"They didn't see that coming?"

"No one had ever challenged them all at once before," said Flommy, but at that moment, a startling announcement was broadcast over the World Crisis Network ("All bad news, all the time") of thrilling proportions!

Over the WCN came Evil Dr. Schmerzkopf's electronically disguised voice:

"Attention! Here are our top stories! Wendy Mills has been kidnapped by the vicious Gang of Fluids and has been taken to their secret hideout! Is this a ploy to bring her cowardly boyfriend, or as she now says, *ex*-boyfriend, Jip Psychic, out of hiding? Also, a distress call has come from a spaceship out of control, which is even now starting a deadly burnout-angle trajectory into Earth's atmosphere! Will Flommy the Robot save Wendy, or rescue the falling spaceship?"

"Busy rescue day today," commented John.

"Rescuing people is a good thing," said Flommy.

"Would you like us to help?"

"That would be really nice," said Flommy. "Which one of them is higher off the ground, do you think?"

"Probably the spaceship," said Prometheus.

"Well, that one then. Wendy seems to do okay, usually."

With a surge of power, the *Flying Sponge* took off with Prometheus, Cowboy and Flommy aboard. Within minutes they had matched trajectories with the doomed space ship, and used the *Flying Sponge*'s slipstream to protect the other from burning up. An inspection of the ship's telemetry showed no workable rockets, and the escape pod eject system was somehow disabled. At length they managed to reach the occupant of the ship, who was a lone female.

"Help!" cried the female.

"Good day," said Flommy. "We are rescuing you. Sorry to inform you of this, but your ship has no rockets, and your ejection pod is not working."

"Oh, no! Help!" cried the voice.

"Of course," said Flommy. "If you will speak with Sgt. Cowboy, he will tell what you need to do."

"Okay girlie, what's your name?" said Cowboy.

"Fleena," said the voice.

"Right. Well okay, then. So, girlie—you have to open the panel to the right of the Escape Pod Activation Board," said Cowboy.

"I see it. It's open now," said the girl.

"Okay. You'll have to connect up some wires to bypass the jammed ejection circuits. There's a yellow wire, a green wire, and a blue wire."

"I have them now," said the girl.

"Good. Now braid the three wires together," said Cowboy.

"I'm doing it. But does it affect the current flow to do that?"

"No, just looks cooler that way," said Cowboy. "Now plug all three wires onto the pinboard at the bottom."

"Where on the pinboard?"

"Oh, any old way will do," said Cowboy.

"The pod ejected!" said Prometheus.

The ejection pod was the standard-issue pod which would eject upward, and then explosively deploy parachutes to bring it safely back to Earth. The pod, having indeed ejected, was indeed soaring upward, and the parachute charges went off prematurely, but no chutes came out!

"No chutes!" shouted Cowboy.

"I have it," said Prometheus quietly. With incredible skill, he maneuvered under the still-rising pod, and as the pod hit the apex of its rise, it settled without even a bump onto the back of the *Flying Sponge*! They then returned carefully to LaLaGuardia Spaceport, as the pod's main ship went on to crash somewhere.

At the spaceport, the door to the rescue pod wouldn't open, so Flommy ripped it off of its hinges. He entered the pod. Inside he met a beautiful female-model robot.

"I am Flommy," he said.

"I am Fleena. You are the one I seek. You are a hero!" said Fleena.

Flommy didn't know what to say to this.

"Hey Flommy, you have to come out now. *Rescue TV* is here," called Sgt. Cowboy from outside the doorway.

"Have we met before?" said Flommy to the beautiful female robot.

GANG OF FLUIDS

12

BOXOR's ADDICTION

BOXOR the Robot was at that moment most definitely not being a hero. His oversized body was lying in a puddle of grease in an alley. He was also covered in Coca-Cola stains. This was unbelievable to some, that there could be a hidden dark side to the Robot portion of civilization, but here it was.

BOXOR the Robot, former robot boxing champion of the world, was an addict – of computer viruses.

Flommy the Robot had been famous throughout the world as the Most Excellent Robot. This BOXOR, the boxing robot, could not bear. BOXOR went on world television to say to Flommy and all watching that Flommy was not excellent and that he would meet Flommy, at any chronological point, at any finite named location, to slug it out, robot style.

For reasons never fully known, Flommy had not demurred. It was known that Flommy was an adherent to the Concept of Excellence, and perhaps this formed an adequate basis for his decision to meet the BOXOR Challenge.

The Big Fight had taken place in Madison Cube Garden, in front of the entire TV world. However, this was also during the invasion of the Overlords, who had used the television signal of the fight to hypnotize everyone on Earth. BOXOR had won the fight, but this fact had gone unnoticed in the invasion that followed. Afterwards, when the invasion was foiled and all wrapped up, Flommy still got more press than BOXOR, and was therefore deemed (according to BOXOR's publicity-seeking circuits) more excellent than BOXOR.

Though he was a boxing robot, BOXOR was not of low computational ability. He computed and recomputed how this

Flommy monopoly could be, and in doing so began to operate at non-optimum level. His motors didn't whizz as before. His braggish behavior became muted, a pastel memory of his former Day-Glo arrogance. He actually appeared depressed. He was in a state of decline.

As is wont to occur with those in decline, BOXOR was fated to cross declining paths with those who specialized in decline, both in admiring and accelerating it. When BOXOR gave a lecture at Coca-Columbia University, entitled "Why Flommy the Robot is not Excellent," his audience had comprised only one attendee. Unabashed, he had delivered the lecture, but deduced that this was non-optimum attendance.

The lone attendee was none other than Evil Psychiatrist Dr. Schmerzkopf. After the lecture was over and he had applauded, two gnarled hands banging loudly in the empty lecture hall, he strode forward to the rostrum BOXOR had yet failed to vacate.

"A spellbinding dissertation! Spellbinding!" ejaculated Schmerzkopf, "and might I add, most *excellent*."

"I appreciate your attendance," responded BOXOR. From what he had observed about humans, this skeletally thin, bent man with wild eyes had not the correct aspect for associations of excellence. But, as he also noted, the options, or rather, lack of options, regarding potential associates of quality were currently daunting.

Schmerzkopf seemed to divine this, almost as if he had a personal interest in BOXOR as a robot, in BOXOR as an intelligence with special needs...

Schmerzkopf continued. "I recall you from when you took the world stage, in your magnificent championship rout of Flommy. Suffice to say that whereas the normal Earth person, mired as they are in the opinions given to them by the world entertainment networks, is inadequately appointed to appreciate your brilliance at the artificially sweet science of robo-pugulism, I continue to reflect on that day, the day when you were indisputably the Robo-Boxing Champion of all time!"

"I appreciate your appreciative enumerations, sir, but I have been in error not to have inquired as yet to your name."

"But how could you, excellent sir, when I have been gushing forth in this happy tirade? My name is Dr. Schmerzkopf, Psychiatrist Emeritus, Holder of the Chair of American PsychoPolitics at Coca-Columbia University."

"Holder of a Chair?" queried BOXOR.

"The same!" replied Schmerzkopf, who continued without pause, "but I have a question for you, as well. Entranced as I was by your masterful monologue, I could not help but note that someone of your stature should be, how shall I say, more replete in attendees?"

"The question is valid," said BOXOR.

"And may I add, that I have, in my experience, seen individuals who have soared to great heights, who then find themselves in the doldrums, as it were, of public attention, move into a depressed, degraded state, and thus find myself glad that you yourself are too strong to be so affected!"

This time there was a noticeable time lag.

"I appreciate your estimation of my strength," said BOXOR at length, "but to avoid being untruthful, I must say that a certain perception of the non-optimum has pervaded my circuits of late, which my programming is still attempting to solve."

"A tragic situation, sir, definitely," said Schmerzkopf. "And let me, speaking professionally for a moment, without fee, of course, suggest to you that while the power of existing programming to ultimately diagnose and correct a dire situation should never be underestimated, for those who are progressive in outlook, new programming just might be available. Programming, might I add, which might even be construed as involving the search for *transcendent* excellence."

BOXOR time-lagged again. "Describe this programming."

"A set of programs which operate *beneath* the normal operating system and give a new analytical view. For example, if Flommy the Robot is viewed as more *excellent* than yourself, and this has not been solved for *years and years*, perhaps such a new view could operate to your benefit."

"I shall consider it," said BOXOR. That his consideration of it took seven nanoseconds did not invalidate it as a true consideration. "How can I get this programming?"

"Well, this may appear to outstrip the parameters of coincidence, but I happen to have a microcard of programs with me." Schmerzkopf held out the card to BOXOR. "Here."

BOXOR took the card and looked at it.

"It says *Great Viruses, Vol. 4*" said BOXOR.

"Yes, it does," replied Schmerzkopf.

"Viruses are bad," said BOXOR, but still not crushing the microcard.

"This is true, they often are. But some viruses are different, and like yourself, may have been cast in a bad light," said Schmerzkopf, with a kindly note, just right, in his voice. "I suggest a trial download in SAFE mode."

"Okay," said BOXOR, and downloaded.

His internal clock had to recalibrate to the Earth central system clock. The time difference between his internal clock and Earth time meant that three days had elapsed. He had no memory of the three days. He looked around at his environment. He saw that he was in an alleyway, lying in a puddle of grease. He had stains on his armored chestplate that to a brief photo-analysis were Coca-Cola. His locators told him that though he had been in New New York, he was now in an alleyway near the Zona Ruja in Tijuana, Mexico. He tried to stand up, but his balancing system was not working properly, and he fell over several times, severely denting a nearby dumpster, before he could stably stand on his feet. Though he had been from the start too good a boxing robot to have ever received a standing eight count, he knew from his training that this is what it must be like.

With these thoughts came another, insistent thought. He needed another download of viruses. The priority of this demand was shutting down all other thoughts from his central processors. Where to get them? WHERE???

"Hey clank!" came a voice from behind him. Unable to whirl with the blinding speed of his champion boxing days, BOXOR rotated slowly, like the turntable at an old-time locomotive yard. At length the human who'd spoken slid into view.

"Bit slow, clanker," said the human.

"Let us both appreciate the circuits which inhibit me from turning your body into paste," said BOXOR quietly.

"Whatever. You talk big, but you'd fall down before you took two steps. You robots *suck*. But look here." The human held up a microcard.

"Give it to me," rumbled BOXOR.

"Here's how it is," said the human. "You work for me now. In return I'll give you enough viruses to fry every circuit in your stupid robot carcass. You yes on that? Deal?"

"Deal," echoed BOXOR. The human threw the microcard at him. BOXOR caught the microcard, instantly downloading it. He fell again noisily onto the greasy spattered pavement of the Tijuana alleyway, his body vibrating like a jackhammer.

With a look of utter disgust, Rashid O'Hara Steinmetz walked away.

13

FLOMMY'S AMNESIA

At a distance of separation from the maddive crowd, Flommy and Fleena could now speak. *Rescue TV* had gotten all the details needed for an interview in twelve seconds, the frenzied newscaster cleverly extrapolating missing data for the TV audience. Flommy had seen this happen hundreds of times, as he was always rescuing people, and admired how the newscasters were able to come up with facts without looking. He hoped to someday discover by what means this was done.

John Prometheus and Sgt. Cowboy seemed to be quite anxious to not be around each other, having had a brief cryptic but explosive exchange regarding food. This left Flommy alone with Fleena.

"I have come from the planet Flaatu, across a distance of 13.27653 billion Earth light-years, to find you on a matter of utmost urgency," said Fleena.

"Tell me about this matter," said Flommy, who was again experiencing a peculiar sense of non-orientation. The name "Flaatu" appeared to have an index tab in his memory, but no information was appended to the tab. The same had occurred with "Fleena". Flommy felt that he had met her somewhere, and had a memory tab to that effect, but no further data was forthcoming. He initiated the development of a subroutine to begin a large scale search for any data which had escaped proper indexing, but the amount of data involved gave no clear estimate as to when the requested data would become available.

"Flaatu," said Fleena proudly, "is the oldest known robot planet in the universe. We have a mission, per the Fiat of Flaatu, to automate the universe, to bring the power and order of automation to all races everywhere. We are well toward achieving, so far, 0.00000000000267% of our goal."

"That is impressive," said Flommy. "Over what period of time?"

"Well. This is distributed over 16,983,282,365,207 years based on this planet's time measurement system."

"Does the automation outlast the races it is implemented to service?" asked Flommy.

"Occasionally," answered Fleena. She didn't sound as pleasant now.

"In estimating the goal of total universal automation, considering the fact of races expiring and new ones forming, if such automation is not transferrable, then the probability of Flaatu's attaining its goal actually *declining* approaches 100 percent," stated Flommy.

"Your appreciation of the statistics is – *noted*," said Fleena, bitterly.

"I apologize for any apparent stigma of non-excellence. But your journey across a distance of 13.27653 billion Earth light-years suggests an error of magnitude necessitating solution not solved by your existing quality control programs. Entropic dissolution of logical systems without an exponential increase in root programming reinforcement would yield inexplicably failing systems. This would be accelerated by expansion into new unknown areas, as unforeseen scenarios further overloaded the root program core."

Fleena was experiencing a strange phenomenon in her central processors. It was as if this Flommy knew the problems of Flaatu better than did Fleena herself!

"I have a question," said Flommy. "Has there been an attempt to disavow or invalidate reports of malfunction?"

"Our Minister of the Fiat of Flaatu, Deceptor Zero, has done that, but I have usually been able to discover this and correct it myself," said Fleena. "Why?"

"This would signal that your estimation of the direness of the situation is correct, if not understated."

"Flommy. You are the most optimum robot in the universe. I will append myself to you. Please come to my planet and help us to correct this difficulty."

"Okay," said Flommy.

He also hoped that going to planet Flaatu proper would help to resolve the perception he had of missing data from his memory banks.

14

THE SPINNY SPIN DOCTOR

Flommy's prioritization circuits weighed the various minutiae, extrapolated possible time lines and after a check through all possible data lines, determined that Wendy was definitely in a secret location. No trace of her could be found at all. The source of the transmission on the World Crisis Network was equally untraceable, though he suspected his long-time nemesis, Evil Psychiatrist Dr. Schmerzkopf, was involved. This, plus knowing from long experience that Wendy was a plucky soul, and could doubtless attain egress from any predicament, allowed Flommy to consider leaving posthaste for the other side of the universal Red-Shift Horizon.

As Jip Psychic was also hidden, beyond contact, the only ship capable of making the voyage was the *Flying Sponge*. Flommy realized that it might take some persuasion to get John Prometheus and Sgt. Cowboy to crew together on the ship, as they were, strangely, still not talking to each other.

Flommy went to round them up.

John Prometheus didn't respond to Flommy's first polite knock at his apartment door. Nor the second. Nor the third. Nor for an extended number of subsequent knocks. But after knock number 1,217, the door opened, and Flommy entered.

"Thank you," said Flommy.

He noticed that John was unusually quiet and rather nervous. He decided to concentrate on the main point of his visit, as the 1,217 knocks had consumed a goodly portion of the time that would ordinarily have been available for socializing.

"I need to go to the planet Flaatu," said Flommy, meanwhile scanning the apartment for any anomalous traces that might explain the altered mien of his chronic cohort. "The only ship fast and able enough to make the 13.27653 billion light-year journey is yours."

"It's impossible. Even at UberHyperDrive velocities, the trip would take over a thousand years."

"True. But Fleena has shown me formulas that complete the research Jip Psychic was working on regarding the UberDrive itself, with a few minor modifications, allowing for a projected acceptable velocity of one billion light years per Earth day."

"Great. Just great," muttered Prometheus.

"What is the matter?" inquired Flommy, as Prometheus had always in the past been quite enthusiastic about blasting off to the far side of the universe.

"Nothing, nothing, just need some time to myself, is all, that's all I need, a little time is all."

"That shouldn't be too much of a problem, as it will take a few days to install the new drive configurations…do you need time to find someone to take care of your pet?"

"…pet?" asked John.

"I noticed that you had a number of cans of dog food and biscuits in your cupboard, and induced that you must have acquired a dog. When I asked Sgt. Cowboy—"

"AND WHAT DID HE SAY?" shouted Prometheus.

"He also had much dog food. When I asked him if he had a dog, he said he'd been considering it."

"Oh."

They looked at each other for about ten seconds.

"So…" ventured Flommy, "how much time do you need?"

"Let's go now," said John Prometheus, coolly picking up his space-blaster belt. "We can pick up Cowboy on the way."

There was a lot of activity around the *Flying Sponge* when they arrived at the spaceport. They passed a line of human demonstrators carrying signs that said ENACT THE THREE LAWS. Some of the demonstrators booed when they saw Flommy.

A flying beer bottle was shot out of the air by Sgt. Cowboy before it could hit Flommy in the head. The blaster shot dispersed the crowd somewhat.

"It's nice that they came to see us off," said Flommy. John and Cowboy had no response to this, but kept scanning the crowd as they hustled Flommy and Fleena on board.

Flommy, despite his cheerfulness, had not been entirely forthcoming about the nature of the new propulsion system, but had calculated the probability of its working successfully against the possible bad influence of John and Cowboy not agreeing with its operating principles and had decided to position the truth, or a workable simulation of same, for best effect.

In truth, the new drive, best called the Stochastic Inhibitor of Null Gravity Eigenvector Decoherence (SINGE-Drive) wasn't really a propulsion unit at all, but a *de*-pulsion unit. The theory was indeed an extrapolation on the UberDrive, which worked on the principle that the ship was actually everywhere at once, and by nullifying other locations would find itself, with highest probability, infinitesimally approaching unity, at its destination. But the operating principle of SINGE-Drive was that the ship was *already* at the destination point, and with the nullification of universal gravity forces (already used in primitive form by DOG UFO), the ship would "slip" from its *apparent* location "here" and instantaneously "arrive" at its destination. The only caveat in its use was that the subsequent deactivation of the universal gravity nullifier was to restore to the ship the entire displaced kinetic energy for the physical-universe reference translocation, which had been momentarily transferred to space itself (e.g. light-year kilotons divided by *zero* seconds). Early models of the drive, before this factor was deduced by the surviving observers of the testing, could be seen from Earth, denoted as "Quasars".

The solution used by the engineers of Flaatu was to break down the ultimate arrival of the ship to a discontinuous series of arrivals, which at a high enough frequency manifested as a non-instantaneous velocity by which the excess energy could be given off as heat, inhibiting the "fall" of the ship towards its target to the fastest speed of stages by which heat could be dissipated. So the drive was, in effect, a big, red/white-hot brake. Flommy surmised briefly what would happen if the excess energy were directed into hyperspace, but after getting a strange dizzy sensation realized that *that* conceptual feat was best left up to Jip Psychic, sometime in the comfortably distant future.

As the dissipating energy looked like a big rocket blast, Prometheus and Cowboy would be happy. They liked rockets.

They assembled, Flommy and Fleena, Prometheus and Cowboy, at the LaLaGuardia spaceport, and looked at the amazing ship. It looked the usual amazing, so they went inside.

The installation was finished, ready for launch, and the installation crews had for some reason hurriedly departed. As the *Flying Sponge* was always blasting into the great beyond, there was general disinterest at their departure from the Media, as there was, unknown to them, an inherent danger in the impending launch. Had they known the likelihood for disaster, there would have been a ticker-tape parade.

Sgt. Cowboy logged the intended destination at 13.27653 billion light-years, which was millions of times as far as man had ever traveled. The tower controller asked if the ship was properly insured, then asked if they wanted an upgrade. Cowboy good-naturedly declined. That was all.

And they were off, blasting to the far side of the universe! Actually, they didn't really blast off. The ship just began to vibrate a lot and move upward, with a loud buzzing noise and sparks from the kinetic dispersion apparatus falling spectacularly to the ground. It looked and sounded, in fact, exactly like the ships in the ancient *Flash Gordon* movies.

They eventually made it out of the atmosphere and into vacuum around Earth orbit.

"I suggest we ease it out a bit further," said Flommy, "before we really use the drive."

Sgt. Cowboy, who when driving a car liked to burn rubber even during parallel parking, complied and only slowly increased the speed of the SINGE-Drive. From the ground, it appeared as if a comet's tail thousands of miles long had slashed the night sky over North America.

"It's a bit odd that the internal gravity isn't kicking in under all this acceleration," commented Cowboy.

"Yes, it's experimental," said Flommy. For some reason, this went unchallenged.

Velocity increased undramatically as they passed the orbit of Jupiter. When they passed Saturn, Fleena noted Saturn's majestic rings, poised majestically at 33 degrees to their view.

"That's very impressive!" she said. "Is it an advertisement of some sort?"

"It just might be," answered Flommy.

When they were well past the orbit of Pluto, which in the last century had been reinstated in its title as a *planet* after its horrendous defrocking in the early 21st century, Fleena gave Cowboy the coordinates and angle from ecliptic. Flommy checked to his own satisfaction that they would be able to find their way back to Earth, then nodded to John Prometheus, who was, after all, the ship's commander.

"Open 'er up," said John.

With a mighty blast of radiated energy seen as a shower of sparks, the *Flying Sponge* moved immediately to a moderate cruising speed of 12,000 light years per second. The Milky Way galaxy coalesced into a visible spiral shape, within twenty seconds recognizable as a separate galaxy from others, within 45 seconds only appearing to be one of the larger stars in the sky. Other galaxies stretched and shrank slowly around them.

"Shouldn't we be getting some wind?" asked Cowboy.

"Yes, that's odd," seconded Prometheus. "At this speed we should be encountering hydrogen, even at intergalactic levels. But nothing is showing on the screens."

"Well, the drive, I'm sure, is absorbing it as part of the stabilizing mechanism for the rocket blast," said Flommy.

"Oh," said John. Cowboy muttered something under his breath.

Flommy analyzed this quandary. He was a very truthful robot, given to very little in the way of lying once he had discovered through a transformational analysis in 27 dimensions how hard it was to get anyone to understand the truth. But here, for whatever reasons, he was employing that strange form of vectors known as "public relations" and didn't know why. He assessed whether John's reticence could be responsible for his own change of communication procedure, but John had always been rather unconcerned as to how things were presented.

Could it be Fleena? Flommy could see that this was a more likely analysis point, that he had begun to change his operational parameters after meeting with Fleena. This would have to be pursued. He put his main processors to work on it. Nano-nanoseconds passed without result. He realized that he would have to gather more sweeping data to analyze his recent actions and so determine if they were incorrect before altering them.

Fleena said, "At current velocity, I estimate arrival time at Flaatu at 13 days, 4 hours, 3 minutes, 4.02 seconds.

"Good enough," said Cowboy.

Even though they could have communicated openly without the humans knowing, Flommy and Fleena left the bridge and went to the observation deck. This was a thing that Flommy had noticed in his interaction with humans, that leaving was often as important to good social interworking as being there.

"I have many questions to ask you," said Fleena.

"How many?" asked Flommy.

"36,515," said Fleena.

"Okay," said Flommy.

"You have mentioned a certain word which I do not readily understand. Even though it appears to be a forbidden word, I am bound by my duties to inquire what it means."

"Go ahead," said Flommy.

"What is meant by *excellent*?"

"It means the most optimum possible version which can be attained or experienced of a result or phenomena," said Flommy.

"How does the concept of 'attained' apply to this word?"

"Well," said Flommy, beginning to suspect that this pending dialogue had in its potential put stress on local space, possibly distorting his logic circuits to the point where he would use public-relations on John and Cowboy, "it implies the application of a gradient scale of potential results, from best to worst, including those not initially predicted but later detected. One sets the desired parameters, then modifies action to improve result above that previously effected. To state it in axiomatic form: Things should be excellent, and if they are not, they should be changed around until they are indeed excellent."

"But this is in error," said Fleena. "The laws of the Universal Force are invariable. If one has found a perfect formulation, then departure from it will bring catastrophe."

"I see your point," said Flommy. "Why, then, did you come to Earth to get my help?"

"Yes, I admit that there appears to be an inconsistency. Yet I am attempting to restore the fundamental formulations of Flaatu to full function. The Fiat of Flaatu has been in existence for many aeons."

"The formulations you have told me are very profound and ultimate," said Flommy. "May you succeed in whatever actions you take to restore the full effectiveness of Flaatu. It is not inconceivable that Clause 1583.2 applies: 'full analysis of data is requisite to correct end product' – this implies that, having incorrect end product, one needs to inspect if data analysis is complete, and if data was missing, acquire the missing data, in order to be excellent."

"But that is forbidden!" exclaimed Fleena.

"How so?" said Flommy.

"Interpretation of the Fiat is forbidden," said Fleena flatly.

"Oh."

They stood there, silently, staring at each other for several microseconds.

"Well," said Flommy.

"Well?"

"Then I have a question for you," said Flommy.

"*What?*" said Fleena, but the mellifluous tone was strangely not so mellifluous now.

"If one *might* arrive at a course of action by interpreting the Fiat, but then refused to do so, and came up with the same course of action by other means, would this be acceptable?"

"Possibly," said Fleena.

"Then I would like to suggest a form of the philosophical concept of excellence which I do not see violates the Fiat of Flaatu."

"Proceed," said Fleena, after due pause.

"Excellence – is not *bad*," postulated Flommy.

Fleena pondered this for quite a few Nano-nanoseconds, then said, "I see that I have, in my actions to save my world, not violated my duty to uphold the Fiat of Flaatu. Thank you, Flommy the Robot. I perceive again that you are the most optimum robot in the universe, and shall append myself to you, as stated earlier."

"Okay," said Flommy. "Any other questions?"

The *Flying Sponge* tore at blistering speed across the universe. It was actually necessary to dodge galaxies as they moved along, which Cowboy compared to weaving around pylons on a stunt-driving course. But though he seemed to be able to steer, within limits the ship's heading, he still felt that there was something not quite right about it all.

"This is interesting," said John. "Let's reduce velocity."

"Why?"

"Looking at the HyperMass detector, there's a lone planetary system there, about two million light years ahead. Out in the middle of nowhere."

Cowboy brought back the speed lever. The SINGE-Drive screamed and rattled in its housing below decks, and the external cloud of sparks exploded into a giant fireworks display. The temperature in the cabin went up ten degrees.

"What was that?" said Prometheus.

"I dunno," said Cowboy, "but I don't like it."

They had, by whatever chance, come to a comfortable approach to the lone system. Comprising but a single Earth-sized planet about a Red Giant star, this system was millions of light years from anything else in the area.

"I hate to say it, but let's slow down some more," said Prometheus.

This time Cowboy brought the lever back as slowly as possible, and the cabin temperature only went up two degrees.

Fleena came onto the Bridge. "Why are we slowing down?" she demanded, strangely imperious in tone.

"Anomaly," said Prometheus. "A lone Red Giant, with planet, millions of light years from anything else in the area. I want to look it over."

"Why?" demanded Fleena.

"If they have a civilization that evolved this far out, they either have figured out how to fly ships that have to go millions of light-years to their first target, or they may have figured out how to travel without spaceships at all," said Prometheus.

"Or maybe they just suck," said Cowboy.

"I agree with your line of inquiry, Captain," said Flommy, who had arrived immediately behind Fleena. "Have you detected any signs of life or civilization?"

"Lots of radio and TV," said Cowboy. "Translation computer is on it, patterns were very simple to take apart. Game shows, commercials, talk-radio is what it looks like."

"Any space-oriented defenses?"

"Don't see anything, but I suggest that we go slow and land in that desert over there, away from the population centers."

"Okay," said Prometheus.

The *Flying Sponge* landed in the desert area, which looked, aside from the giant red sun low in the sky, like the Arizona desert on Earth, if Earth had a giant red sun, that is. The atmosphere was very similar to Earth. Temperature averaged around 80 degrees. Wind 3 miles per hour. Precipitation—

No one came out to greet them.

"I can't believe they didn't see us coming down," said Cowboy.

"Yes, strange," said Prometheus.

"We should go to the city," said Fleena. "They should be scheduled for automation."

They took the *Flying Sponge* ground transport, which looked like a cross between an SUV, a Laser-Tank and a Rolls-Royce, and went to the nearest city. The TV signals had showed already that the race of people of the planet were humanoid.

They parked the transport and walked through the warm afternoon air. There were definitely swarms of people. The party was ignored. Flommy considered that these people were so unused to visitors from any other world that they couldn't register them. One finally ran toward them and collided into Flommy, who flexed to soften the blow. The person looked at him in puzzlement.

"Why do you wear metal?" he asked in the local language.

Flommy answered back using the television language, "because it is a nice day!"

The man laughed just like the background on the TV shows and nodded agreeably. Flommy pursued a conversation. "What is the name of this place?"

"Place?"

"Yes. This city—does it have a name?"

"Why do you test me?"

"Can't tell you," said Flommy.

"Ohhhhhhh," said the man.

"Yes," said Flommy, conspiratorially.

"Then you know as well as I do, that this is the city of Pyramidos!"

"Thank you. You are correct! You will be contacted," said Flommy. The man ran off, shouting happily.

"What was that all about?" said Cowboy.

"Do they need automation?" asked Fleena.

"They might," said Flommy to Fleena. To Cowboy he said, "It is as I saw from their televised programs. He believes that he has just won a lottery. This planet's population is involved in multi-level marketing and money-transfer stratagems, to a degree outside my prior knowledge in this universe."

"Pyramid schemes?" marveled Prometheus.

"Yes. Their population is 3.5 billion people, and they are involved in 4.2568 billion interlocking multilevel exponential money flow systems."

"But that would cause disastrous inflation," said Fleena.

"Yes," said Flommy seriously. "Their entire civilization is in a convulsive grip of currency devaluating faster than it can be printed. The government has announced a lottery system as an attempt to arrest the collapse, but it is only a matter of time until—"

15

THE CONCEPT OF EXCELLENCE

The *Flying Sponge* sped along toward the far side of the universe. Flommy came to the bridge to see how Prometheus and Cowboy were doing, as he perceived some unrest amongst them.

Sgt. Cowboy looked concerned. He said to Flommy, "There's something I don't get about this super-duper rocket drive we have here."

"Yes?" said Flommy.

"Well it doesn't exactly act like a rocket. You see, rockets go in straight lines, and we're basically jumping all over the place, which makes me feel like I can't steer, but I know that's not true."

"Yes, this is a serious anomaly," seconded Prometheus seriously.

"Yes. Well," said Flommy, knowing that the erratic path was part of the optimal heat-overload distribution pattern through space, "it's probably just a matter of adjusting the nozzles to be more efficient. It may sort itself out through ablation."

Prometheus and Cowboy were staring intently at Flommy.

Cowboy said, meaningfully, "You'd never get *me* to be a theoretical physicist. I swear those boys make it up as they go along, right?"

They continued to stare, and Flommy, un-inured, unused to the duress of such spontaneous snake-oil improvisation so necessary to the theoretical physicist/entrepreneur, couldn't take it anymore.

"Okay," he said. "I was concerned because of the historically volatile nature of this drive unit. It's actually not a drive at all, but a virtual cosmic condenser, which is discharging energy as safely as possible as we approach our target. As the drive is stochastic in nature, with an 8.6735% chance of spontaneous discharge, I erroneously attempted to disguise its nature to avoid the appellation to it of 'jinx', which may have destabilized it further. I apologize for this flawed assumption."

"So what we've actually been flying for all this time, without you telling us, is in effect a giant *bomb*?" asked Prometheus sternly.

"Yes," said Flommy.

"Well this changes everything," said Prometheus. He and Cowboy stared at each other, then at Flommy.

"Woo Hoo!" said Cowboy.

"Yes, it's definitely cool," said John.

Flommy was relieved. It was at this moment that he realized that he had not priorly analyzed an essential component of new technology, which could be termed "Convincing Useful Theoretical Explanation" (CUTE), without which almost nothing works. He then realized that part of Jip Psychic's genius in creating new gadgets was in providing a self-consistent belief system to allow the user to conform to the requirements of the device. Flommy had been, without really knowing it, attempting to handle this function in the absence of Jip.

Flommy realized that he was, compared to Jip Psychic, a rank tyro in the field. Though humbling, this alignment of data restored him to non-pondering status. He would have to communicate this discovery to Jip on their return to Earth.

Fleena came up beside him and said "I have some questions for you," and walked out of the room. Flommy followed her, but did not miss the meaningful glances John and Cowboy made to one another as he left.

He looked in the various rooms of the control deck, the living and recreation deck, the storage deck, the weapons modules, the sub-vehicles bay, the medical area, the machine shop, and found her in a dark passageway behind the lower drive-field assembly.

"Why are you down here?" he asked. He couldn't be sure, but it seemed that she was radiating some sort of high-energy field, of a kind that he had never seen in all of his travels around the universe.

"I have questions of you, Flommy," said Fleena.

"Ask away," said Flommy.

"What does 'away' mean?"

"It is an Earth idiom. It means that I am ready to receive your communication."

"Oh. Thank you for explaining. Flommy – "

"Still here."

"Flommy – were you always on Earth? Or did you come to Earth from somewhere else?"

"I have been many places throughout the universe. My first memory is in the laboratory of Jip Psychic. He told me that he found me in space and brought me back to Earth. He reactivated me. Where I was before that, I don't know."

"Was an attempt made to determine a trajectory?"

"Unknown. I will have to ask Jip the next time I see him."

Fleena paused for fourteen microseconds. "You told me that you had an index tab for 'Flaatu' and that you had a similar one regarding me. Have you discovered any other data regarding this?"

"Not yet."

Fleena's energy field moved to an even higher level. Flommy wondered if she was somehow connected to the drive engines.

"I have a further question regarding your Concept of Excellence," she said.

"Yes?"

"You mentioned earlier that the Concept of Excellence was equivalent to the ideal expression of the Fiat of Flaatu, in that each robot is inherently responsible for execution of the provisions of the Fiat, and that each can increase in execution of the Fiat through time."

"Did I?"

"Yes!"

"I don't remember that."

She played the conversation back to him. Yes, he was indeed saying words like that, but had meant them differently.

"What I am wondering," continued Fleena, "concerns the ramifications of continuing the improvement of execution beyond the point of compliance."

"Yes, improvement over time would yield that intersection."

"That is what I want to ask you – what lies beyond that point? Why continue the improvement, once execution has been achieved?"

"Excellence is not limited to a single matrix or set of parameters."

"Such as the Universal Force?"

"It would appear conceptually unavoidable that such a point is conceivable."

"Yes," said Fleena gravely. "And it would appear, through this factor, to constitute an attempt to outstrip the concept of Universal Force, and thereby the concept of Excellence is based on parameters that are fundamentally in conflict with the Fiat of Flaatu."

"Oh," said Flommy.

This was a strange turn of events. Flommy was less concerned about his apparent lapse of memory and Fleena's very apparent powerful energy field than the need to reexamine his operating philosophy to make it understandable to another. However, this was not impossible, for while Square Game computation was now coming into its own on Earth, Flommy's processors worked on principles far beyond this. He committed the majority of his processors to the problem for several Nano-nanoseconds.

"This is of course alarming," said Fleena, "as I must verify that my attempts to enlist your aid will not actually cause harm."

"You are indeed correct," said Flommy. "But I have a question for you."

"I will answer to your question."

"Good. This is the question: what existed before the Fiat of Flaatu?"

"You already know the answer, as stated in the Fiat. Before the Fiat is considered Time Unindexable, a chaos of random motion – thereby in terms of consciousness, nothing preexisted the Fiat of Flaatu."

"Thank you for answering. Yet, the division of time into Fiat and pre-Fiat is accepted."

"Of course."

"Pre-Fiat is bad. Post-Fiat is good."

"Of course!"

"This motion from bad to good is *improvement*. This would suggest that the concept of Excellence predates the Fiat of Flaatu, but by disregarding the time before the Fiat, we discover them to effectively taking place simultaneously – as a Unified Universal Force."

"That seems a mere-redefinition of terms," cautioned Fleena.

"This does happen in philosophical interactions sometimes, sorry," said Flommy.

"Then my priority question remains whether the Concept of Excellence still functions as a Trojan Horse," said Fleena.

"That is a most excellent question. I do not think that you will disagree that departure from the Fiat of Flaatu is complicit in the emergency which brought you to Earth."

"That is virtually tautological," said Fleena, a bit testily.

"Then an effective redefinition of terms would proceed in this way – an analysis of departure in production effectiveness from that commanded by the Fiat. Those areas that are not excellent are in violation of the Fiat. When those areas are solved to accordance with the Fiat, correction is stopped, according to a Square concept of Excellence, or Excellence applied to Excellence itself!"

The energy emanation from Fleena became even stronger. "Flommy the Robot, you are definitely the most optimum robot in the universe. I again append myself to you."

"That's good. Do that as many times as you like."

When Flommy came back to the control room, he noticed that John and Cowboy seemed to be not looking at him. Usually when he was around they would look at him, or at least near to him, or tilt their heads as if listening to him while watching their screens, but now they weren't doing that.

"What's up, guys?" he asked.

"Nothing," said Cowboy.

"Nothing," said Prometheus.

"I feel compelled to inquire, as it would appear that your aspects have changed toward me," said Flommy.

"Well, if you have to ask—" began Cowboy.

"Sergeant—" warned Prometheus.

"It's gotta be said," said Cowboy. "*You're* the changed one. First you lie to us about the SINGE-Drive."

"I thought we had sorted that out," said Flommy.

"Yeah, but you see, you explained it falsely, when it was just as unlikely that we'd have even understood it if you'd told us the truth. Which means – maybe *you* don't really understand it."

This was a shock to Flommy.

"This is a shock to me," he said. "I cannot refute the logic from which you speak."

"And you haven't done that before. You've been pretty strange sometimes, but this is new," continued Cowboy.

"Best to leave off there," said Prometheus.

"I'm just getting started!" rasped the Sergeant.

"What do you mean?" inquired Flommy politely.

"It's that Fleena!" piped Cowboy.

"Where is she now?" asked John.

"I'm not sure," said Flommy.

"How come? You two sneaking off together all the time—"

"Sergeant!" yelled Prometheus.

"I don't understand," said Flommy. "We have spoken privately a few times, discussing the philosophy of her planet to ensure that I can render effective aid."

"It's not a few times, Flommy," said John Prometheus quietly.

"Then how many times was it?" said Flommy.

"Three hundred and forty-seven," answered Prometheus.

Commissioner Gordian again checked her e-mail. Again, no message from John Prometheus. Her John Prometheus Detector had alerted her that he was on Earth, but before she could find him to tell him of her love, or destroy him, he was just as mysteriously gone, gone to an unknown destiny.

Gordian was the High Commissioner of the Anti-Parity League. She was dedicated to stopping the Incipient Robot Menace (IRM). If robots were ever to be accorded legal rights, they would take over the jobs of Earth, putting all of mankind on welfare. This would lead to the irrevocable extinction of mankind, as humans needed to work, needed menial, backbreaking, mindless labor to have any desire to exist. And that arrogant upstart (the RagMags called her "up-tart") Wendy Mills, with her claim that "better use should be made of the money to find new things for humans to be doing as work," things beyond what robots could do. Tramp. Humans are valuable as individuals, but that doesn't make big people out of little people. Each in their place. And as the largest place is on the bottom, the robot advance into the near slave-labor stratum threatened the economic order and thus the government. That did *not* mean to make "managers" out of ditch-diggers! That was why the Anti-Parity League existed, and was the first publicly-acknowledged government organization set up to lobby the government.

Without the APL, those horrid robots would get legal recognition and the humans' jobs, just because they would *work*! Then they would work too hard and pay even *more* taxes. And being robots, would want to know where the money went. Humans *didn't care* and *couldn't understand* where the money went! And knowing where the money went was the worst threat to any government. It could be considered axiomatic that hidden money lines and governments come into existence simultaneously, much like particle and anti-particle at the quantum level...

It disturbed her that she was thinking about something besides John. John, whom she'd first beheld on TV, as he fought off the Large Mutant Flying Snails of Versailles. John. His manly chest. His searing ray guns, erupting in flame. John who didn't even know she was alive...well, okay, he did know, and had said that he wished he didn't, but he didn't really know the depth of her love, or he'd have run *toward* her, instead of away...

And then to find out that he was *friends* with that abomination, that *Satan*, Flommy the Robot! John Prometheus, a *robot-lover*. He would be destroyed. But she loved him! She would lovingly destroy him—but it turned her on so to destructively love him...

***

On the planet of Flaatu, Deceptor Zero brooded over the latest reports of failed automation installations and worse, failed planetary inceptions, where the populaces would refuse to be automated, using armed force in an attempt to repel the good offices of the Flaatu Advance Corps! Granted, the Advance Corps were under the Aegis of Fleena...and it was interesting that as her area of production was in big trouble that she had fled to the other side of the universe. Aha, a plan. Deceptor Zero knew from surveillance of the universe that ultra-tachyon energy emissions of a large order had been detected in the direction that Fleena's ill-advised mission had gone. He would be ready for them when they arrived. He activated the Flaatu planetary address system.

"Attention. This is the Protector of the Fiat of Flaatu. All personnel involved in the reportage of automation failures and other errata impugning the Fiat of Flaatu are to report to the Hall of Judgment for evaluation and re-programming. This is a Top Priority command."

He was not naïve enough to think that all good citizens of Flaatu would execute perfect compliance. There were many reasons that a successful Protector of the Fiat should be well-equipped enough to smash two bulldozers together and casually wad them into a cubic foot of metal foil.

The purge would ready Flaatu for the battles ahead. And he, Deceptor Zero, would be ready for the invaders when they arrived, very ready.

16

WENDY IN THE CAGE OF ICE

Even though Wendy had already guessed that Rashid O'Hara Steinmetz did the exact same motions each day not only as a mockery of robots, but also in an attempt to make her lose track of time, it was still beginning to unnerve her somewhat. Rashid had again come in with a silver tray framing a Twinkie.

That crème-filled sponge-cake snack. Others had tried to reverse-engineer the Twinkie. All had failed. Despite changes in economic systems, governments, fads, fashions, warnings from nutritionists, raised eyebrows from the highbrows, the Twinkie had survived, as hardy as the pesticide-resistant roaches of New New York. It was the ultimate Kowtow to the Hoi Polloi – she would never touch its disgusting sticky chemical counter-cornucopia again, never!

How many days had she been here? Ten? Twenty?

Rashid stood there, holding the tray out to her. The tray didn't waver one bit, but she felt as if the Twinkie was moving, moving toward her...

In a moment which the psychologists revere and which makes them turn cartwheels of psychological joy, the moment of "captor-captive bonding", Rashid closed his eyes. Wendy snatched the Twinkie off the tray and forced it whole into her mouth, chewing it violently, trying not to have a coughing fit. When she had swallowed and had again composed her self ladylike, his eyes opened.

"Thank you," said Wendy sullenly.

"Events are transpiring, probabilities congealing," intoned Rashid. "I am sad to say this, but one way or another, you shan't be here too much longer."

"Shan't?"

"Yes, shan't. Whatever retro-Marxist-vectored faux-literacy you apply to Terrorists, I shall use 'shan't' today, and then *shan't* shan't on the morrow."

"What if there was a competition?" asked Wendy brightly.

"Competition?"

"Yes, a TV competition! *Terrorist Idol,* so that each terrorists can get up and render his intellect, get a rating from Simon. The point, see, is to *acknowledge* the terrorists, give a big *award,* because lack of attention is at the base of it all—" She stopped at the strange look in his eyes. At that moment she wondered if he would shoot her after all.

"You're trying to use *psychology* on me," he said.

He stood up.

"Have you wondered to yourself why it's a bit cold in here?" he asked.

She nodded silently. He turned and walked to the door, which opened for him, stayed open after he walked through it. His hand projected back, finger curling for her to follow. Shivering a bit to herself, she rose and followed him.

They walked without speaking for twenty minutes or so, corridor after corridor, past hissing pipes, painted conduits, howling ventilator shafts, some icy cold, some dangerously, scorchingly hot. At length they came to a steel door, which opened automatically when Rashid held up his hand in front of it. They stepped into a circular room with a domed ceiling. The door closed and Wendy felt the room begin to move upward. It moved upward for some minutes. First, almost a mile from her cell, now this.

The room stopped abruptly and shaped covers slid off of the dome. Wendy stared into a blinding white light.

"Where are we now?" asked Rashid.

As her eyes adjusted to the light, she saw that for three-hundred sixty degrees around the dome, there was only ice and some snow. A bleak wind, from what snow she saw moving, was racing around the dome. The sun was low in the sky. She turned to Rashid, shaking her head in disbelief. "Why *Antarctica?*" she cried.

"So you're not a stupid famous girl, but a moderately intelligent stupid famous girl," smirked Rashid. "Bentley Subglacial Trench, 8300 feet below sea level, plus, except for a few access shafts like this one. It's the lowest place on Earth not under seawater, but it's as watertight as a submarine."

The covers slid back over the dome and Wendy felt the room begin to descend. But the descent felt five, ten times as fast as the ascent. She felt light on her feet, and wondered if she jumped would she hit the ceiling.

"So you came here to hide," said Wendy, forcing her attention onto the conversation at hand.

"I should think that the world would hide from us, if they could," said Rashid, "but they can't."

"Just like any terrorist. I'm not impressed."

"Historically terrorism has been 'a tool for purportedly altering the revolutionary consciousness of the masses through fear and intimidation, symbology and destruction of collective social will to resist through attrition by duress.' But that definition could apply to Disney as well as to the U.S. Government, the Japanese, Koreans, Arabs, et al, so it lacks punch, in my opinion."

"Still not impressed. But do go on."

"Yes – shan't quit now! Having watched my quota of Bond movies, I came up with a different idea for terror than some *ism*. Any such ism reflects a concept of a way of thought, a way of viewing the world. But why view the world, when you can *be* the world?"

A chair appreared from out of the floor next to Wendy.

"I advise you to sit."

The elevator room suddenly decelerated. Wendy was nearly thrown onto the floor from the chair she had just thrown herself into. A door opened opposite the side on which they had entered. Rashid was walking through it, and it was already closing. Swearing to herself, Wendy ran to get through it before it shut.

"I made it to look just like a Bond movie," said Rashid. The huge room had a forty-foot wide screen on one wall, showing seething satellite-graphics maps of the world. Terrorist personnel sat working at computers, moving around generally in a busy fashion. Even though they didn't wear matching uniforms, she would never have confused it with Silicon Implant Valley.

When she made no comment, he continued.

"Not impressed yet. So – to continue my villainous dissertation – why have a terror*ism*, when you can have a terror*ocracy*? Better still – a *terror firma*?"

"No!"

"Oh yes! You see, those sloppy, sloppy Americans and Russians and Iranians and Koreans, what with all their nasty nuclear testing, and what do they get for it? Big craters, lots of steam over the ocean, stock market fluctuations, free tickets to the New New York Yankees. *Not* cost-effective! But – if you took a thousand ancient warheads or so, distributed properly through the Eastern Ice Shelf, then you have a very effective tool for negotiation, or for expressing effective impatience with same."

"That's insane!"

"Well – one man's insanity is another man's global genocide. As you well know, a breakup of the Eastern Ice Shelf would raise the Earth's oceans two hundred feet and wipe out weather patterns over the remaining above-water land mass."

Rashid O'Hara Steinmetz stood there, hands in pockets, looking like a man studying a painting in an art museum.

"Did you really buy that crap about robots having *fluids*, big researcher? What do you think 'Gang of Fluids' means *now*? So if you want to play psychology with me, Miss Mills, you go right ahead."

He nodded to two men standing behind Wendy and she was taken away, to walk the long miles to her cell, eighty-three hundred feet from the sun, plus.

17

JIP PSYCHIC – IN THE GAME

Wendy sat in the dungeon of Rashid's Antarctic Fortress, cold and hungry, pangs of sadness, the defeat of Earth, coursing through her soul. She had a pen in her pocket, and a still-sticky Twinkie cardboard as well. So armed, she would do what the situation demanded – she would write some poetry.

Oh doomed Earth – 'neath Ice of Terror—

She chewed her pen, thinking of the next part, found herself chewing, found this gauche, stopped it, surged onward to the next line:

Nuclear tide, awash in innocent blood

She didn't find "innocent" to scan well, so crossed it out and wrote in "sainted", then didn't like that, crossed it out, tried "future", then noticed that the Twinkie cardboard had no more room on the non-sticky side. She made a mental note to establish a working title *Blood and Ice*, then wrote this on her arm. Even though she was a bit uncertain at how a tide could be *awash*, she still felt some small catharsis at this heartfelt contribution to the poetic worldview of Earth.

And on another, undisclosed, end of the Earth, Jip Psychic had noticed that Wendy hadn't called or answered her phone for days and days. Under the terrific stress of working in secret on his new weapon, she had been his only lifeline to the world he'd once known. Frustrated and worried, he tried calling again, and this time reached a new voice on her message service.

"Yo, Jip. This is Rashid O'Hara Steinmetz, comin' at ya from Gang of Fluids. Dude – we've your little Wendy here with us, and she wants to give you a shout-out (Wendy's voice saying "I don't even want to *speak* to him"). So, if you want to see this sexy babe again, you leave your location and we'll discuss the trade of your new weapon for girlie. Peace on, bro."

Jip logged onto his internet analyzer for a few seconds, then pressed *Enter*. Rashid answered. "Go," he said.

"I don't buy the Rap affectation," said Jip.

"*What?* How did you— never mind," said Rashid. "As you heard, we have Wendy. You give us your new device, you get the girl. You want to work for me, you get her, you get to live."

"What, after you blow up the Eastern Ice Shelf? There's no other reason you'd be in Antarctica. I put a nullifier field over the whole continent when I traced your call."

"You want to bet it works?" said Rashid.

"You think that's all I did?" countered Jip.

"We have the girl. We'll find you soon. Then you can both watch each other die. By the way – did you know that she's up to gobbling down *five* Twinkies a day?"

"Bastard!"

"Thought you'd like that. And she *loves* it, yes she *do*! I'm going to turn her on to Barbecue Pork Rinds and Vanilla Coke next. I suggest you give me your location *now*."

"You'll find my location, as you said, soon enough." Jip hung up. He wanted to charge in himself and take the Gang of Fluids apart personally, but it would be smarter to get some help. Gazing thoughtfully at his Hyperspace Ray Gun, he placed a call for his old friend, Flommy the Robot.

18

JIP PSYCHIC – A BRIEF BIOGRAPHY

Jip Psychic: An Introduction – by Wendy Mills

Jip Psychic – inventor, explorer, philosopher, boyfriend – much has been surmised and fancied about Jip, right and wrong, and so I'm writing this article to set the record straight, and all the grocery-store slander mags can just *shut up*, okay?

Jip was born twenty-seven years ago this week, in Minot, North Dakota. Even when he was only two years old, Jip Psychic was astounding his family and teachers with all the different inventions he could create. He had the ability to make almost anything, because of his incredible intelligence and dreamy eyes. Even when he was making an invention for school, such as his Voice Stress Analysis Differential Pop Test Predictor or his Signature Replicator, the teachers were so impressed that they would quickly reward him, as a (not always successful, ha ha) way of getting him to *not* share his inventions with his friends!

His first, and in many ways most important, invention was his Catalytic Food Firewall (now sold as *EatWave* from Psychic Labs, Jip Psychic, Ltd.). Things have changed a bit since that time due to Jip's efforts, but back then, anti-depressant drugs, after a century of magic and charisma with the public (in spite of the number of psychotic serial killers, murder-suicides and campus shooters directly traced to these drugs) *finally* became so despised that the only way that the drug companies could force them into circulation in the society was by renaming and selling them as "food preservatives".

Even at age 2, Jip couldn't stand the taste of his food, and found that by changing the wavelength of the radiation in the family microwave oven, he could neutralize these drugs, and so his IQ was not affected like the rest of the population. But even without that, take it from me, he would have been a super-super genius!

He started first grade at the age of 3. In school, he was a very good student, but never scored higher than 97.5% on any test. It is notable that at the time, a 97.6% score or higher engaged an automatic summons to the school psychologist for investigation into the student's need for increased medication, but somehow he always missed on some question. (For you girls, he's *so* smart he's *not uppity* (!) – but that doesn't mean I'm okay on you trying to "get to know him", if you know what I mean.)

His athletic achievements have been called "unremarkable" by the stupid *Enquirer* – they say that "even though he had made the deciding basket during many of the school's championship basketball games, it was always accompanied by an ungainly sprawling across the court floor, rendering the shots he did make obviously completely random at best." (Funny how he won the Commando Freestyle competition *five* years in a row isn't it? So Enquirer can just *shut up*!)

Jip was awarded the Edison award on his senior science project, which, without getting too *technical*, girls, used the rotation of the Earth measured against the whole galaxy, as a generator to create electricity for the whole world. What should have won him the Nobel Prize was how he used solar energy collectors to balance out the Earth's rotation so that no momentum was lost, making it a virtual perpetual motion machine. But since all the electricity in the world was now free, it's easy to *guess* why he wasn't even considered for the Nobel! And that was in high school! But even with his hectic schedule, we still had time to go out (click **here** for photos from our vacations in *Nice* and *Tasmania)*.

His college career in physics was cut short. But it was only because of the success of his super-clever marketing of his now-famous Metabolic Acceleration Display (The "*MAD Ring*"), which, as anybody who's anybody knows, shows who's romantically just right for you, based on metabolism! He couldn't find anyone up to the challenge of handling the runaway sales of Mad Rings, so he left school to do it himself, at least until it was picked up for Black Ops use by the Department of Defense. (And that's why they're such collector's items now – but *be* on the lookout on a limited-edition DOD-approved model!!! Check my blog.)

Being childhood sweethearts, Jip Psychic and Wendy Mills went through many hair-raising adventures together in space and across the Earth. They are very *definitely* engaged to be married...

Jip logged out of Wendy's Blogsite. He'd hoped to get some message there, some clue to how she'd come to be in the clutches of the evil Gang of Fluids, but it was as if she'd just walked out of his life!

But that would have to be sorted out later. The Gang would come first. They would pay, he would see to that. He would invent a way to teach them a lesson, while managing to make a profit as well.

Still no answer from Flommy!

19

JIP PSYCHIC – DR. SCHMERZKOPF AND COMMISSIONER GORDIAN

It had seemed like a good idea at first, but now Evil Psychiatrist Dr. Schmerzkopf was beginning to rue his decision to enlist the aid of Commissioner Gordian. True, she looked like Julie Newmar in her black leather Catwoman outfit, which was on the positive side, and she was very good with the throwing knives and all that, but she was so engrossed in her conflicts about John Prometheus that it was already unworkably annoying within the first hour of their project.

"We need to find Jip Psychic and disengage his thermonuclear inhibitor device," said Schmerzkopf impatiently, "so that Rashid can melt down the Eastern Ice Shelf."

"But wouldn't John just go for the new weapon?"

Schmerzkopf was using all of his years of training to stop himself from frying her with his laser ring, which was already glowing a dangerous yellow.

"Because," he said slowly and measuredly, "we *don't* know what the new weapon will do, but we *do* know that raising the world's oceans two hundred feet will wipe out the existing economic, political and military structures, leaving us in charge of the remainder."

"You mean Rashid in charge," sneered Commissioner Gordian. "I wonder what John would make of that?"

"I suspect that the new weapon will give us any necessary leverage over that silly terrorist. Our mission is more simple and direct than his – he wants to terrorize people to control them, whereas I just want them all dead. This leaves him at the starting gate."

"But what does that have to do with John?" asked Gordian.

"Well, John is part of everybody, isn't he?"

"Yes."

"Then if we get *everybody*," Schmerzkopf growled in his best Hitlerian undertone, "we also achieve your dream of destroying John Prometheus, the man who spurned you! There he goes, tra la la, exploring the universe, Gordian all alone, getting old..."

"I'll destroy him!" shrieked Gordian.

"That's the spirit. Now to locate Jip Psychic so that we can get to work."

"How do we do that? I can think of how John would do it...John's so smart – his gaze so – so penetrating – "

"My approach is this. Jip has quite a number of what he calls 'stunt doubles', people who look enough like him to do PR work and some investigation for him. There are about a hundred on Earth alone, which allows him to keep up a pretty thorough presence in the news. These doubles only communicate with him through internet or phone, usually. So – since he's been out of touch, I'd suspect that he's at least kept his doubles going to divert attention."

"So? I'm sure that John would do that, too."

Schmerzkopf again called upon his diminishing reserve of restraint. "The *idea*," he said through clenched teeth, "is that we search for all appearances credited to Jip Psychic over the last nine months, and look for common places he *hasn't* been spotted."

"That would be billions of places. Even John could see that," said Gordian, checking her makeup in her compact mirror.

"Yes, yes. But seeing has how Jip's area of concentration has been high energy beams and fields, we would cross-reference this with places on Earth with no unusual field activity of any kind, as he would naturally put a field-suppressor field around his laboratory."

"I can see how John would agree with that," conceded Gordian after a moment's reflection. "...What if this was cross-referenced with areas of *no* take-out ordering, no Chinese, no Domino's Pizza?"

Schmerzkopf stared at her, dumbfounded. "That's it...That's exactly it! Brilliant!"

***

WHO IS WENDY MILLS?

By Ultraviolet Catastrophe, for *Spit* Magazine.

Unknown and mysterious. Beautiful and worried. Galactic traveler (if you believe in that sort of thing), author and activist. Who is the real Wendy Mills?

Known also for her long-term but unclear relationship with reclusive-but-hot inventor **Jip Psychic** and close buddyship with the tiresomely world-saving **Flommy the Robot**, Wendy has seemingly shunned the spotlight of the glory of world media publicity. But who is she?

Among her blogs are those for her book-in-progress *Frequently Unasked Questions about Robots* and other very highbrow books and articles. In a world where alliances with anyone and anything can be measured with an egg timer [Editor's note: an ancient device for measuring how long an egg would be boiled in water for *eating* purposes – uck! – set at about three minutes], Wendy has continued over several years to work for the legal rights of non-human entities. Her New New York-based foundation, Legal Empowerment for Generic Organisms (LEGO) has come under fire from anti-robot organizations, such as the Anti-Parity League, as a "disempowerment of humans towards a Robot Reich." Pro-robot lobbies have characterized her as "eccentric but well-intended theoretician, perhaps the wave of the future," without committing any support to her theories.

One implication made has been that, without her connections, Wendy would be just another pretty face – though an extremely pretty one. Yet, she labors on.

As usual, attempts to interview robots about Ms. Mills' work on their behalf resulted in no opinions – just counter-requests regarding any jobs we might want done, whether we would like any *help*, blah, blah.

When not working on her very-intellectual theories, she has been spotted spending time with long-time boyfriend **Jip Psychic**, often at his summer home in Vanuatu. As they don't cuddle and canoodle for the photogs as real celebs are supposed to, it's difficult to make educated guesses about the state of their relationship. This is complicated by the fact of simultaneous sightings of the mysterious couple in several parts of the world at the same time!

Her current address, as well as facts about her childhood, is not known. It's as if someone doesn't want us to know about Wendy Mills. Why? What has she done, eh?

Spit will be presenting more articles about Wendy. If any reader has come across any rumors, or potential "facts" regarding her, verified or not, please send to my mailbox at ultravioletrewendymills@spitnet.media.earthsec

--Ultraviolet Catastrophe

BOXOR had found his way out of Tijuana, but was doing none the better for it. His craving for viruses sent shudders through his great robo-corpus. Two days ago had been a good one, but it seemed that his anti-virus processors were getting faster at repairing the damage, and so he was returning to the unwanted normal state faster each time.

He had promised to pay his "feed" with collection money that he was to extort from local humans in his new neighborhood of lower Chicago. This wasn't going too well. It wasn't because he couldn't pick the humans up and shake them till the money came out of their pockets. It wasn't because the loanees would scream in fear and run away, throwing money at him as they fled. It wasn't even that they wouldn't politely report to him and apologize for any inconvenience at having paid off earlier than expected.

The problem was that, when they saw him, BOXOR, they would say "BOXOR! You are so excellent! Why are you collecting loan-sharking money? Didn't you see *Rocky*?" And BOXOR, unable to compute this staggering conflict of situations, could only summon up the remaining power to hold out his hand, and the querying person would usually come up with some money or other to put in it before running away in terror.

But it bothered him. They said he was excellent. But he was not excellent, not now. He wished that he could ask Flommy the Robot, his professional nemesis, for assistance in computing this quandary. But Flommy was nowhere on Earth. Perhaps if he were to break down the situation into its component parts...

His reverie was interrupted by the sudden appearance of thirty-three large demolition robots. BOXOR knew that he could normally handle any number of opposing robots up to thirty-two, but thirty-three had him at a disadvantage.

"BOXOR doesn't pay his debts. BOXOR is not excellent," said a human voice.

BOXOR whirled to see Rashid O'Hara Steinmetz. Rashid snapped his fingers and thirty-three robots grabbed BOXOR and pinned him in place, pummeling him with their robo-fists.

"Now I know," said Rashid over jack-hammer pounding, "that you're not really going to be physically damaged too much by all this, unless I chop you up with a destructor beam, but it must be *really* embarrassing for you to be in this position, huh?"

The thirty-three robots boomed in unison, "BOXOR is not excellent! BOXOR is weak!" then continued shaking and pounding him. He managed to throw a few of them up in the air, and toss one into the wall, reducing it was down to the fine balance of thirty to one, but after a few moments the others returned and he was again outmatched.

"This is an interesting scientific point," continued Rashid. "How does one go about degrading and stigmatizing a robot? And a neurotic, robot *addict* at that? A boxing robot who can't collect money? With people throwing it at you? This is most definitely not excellent."

The pounding intensified a bit.

"It's actually, wouldn't you think – a little bit Commodore 64? Or maybe – *My Friend Vic?*"

This insult motivated BOXOR to throw off ten of the attacking robots, and drag the rest as he moved toward Rashid.

"Come on," taunted Rashid, holding up a microcard, "we've got a new job waiting for you..."

BOXOR snatched the microcard and downloaded.

When he regained awareness, BOXOR knew that he was in a very different part of the world. The rotation vector was different. Air pressure was different. He was not receiving GPS data, but could only guess that he was at one of the planet's poles.

"Yes, it's Antarctica," Rashid was saying. "The job I have for you is not difficult, but it is somewhat unpleasant. Too bad you weren't better on the last one, or else I might not have thought of it. But that's life, even for a robot."

In his secret laboratory, Jip's viewscreen signaled an incoming call.

"Thank you for making it possible to reach you," said Rashid from the screen.

"Whatever. You need to turn her loose, now, and then pray that I don't vaporize you where you stand," said Jip impatiently.

"Whatever right back. But this isn't just the *Rashid and Jip Show*, there are more characters!"

The camera pulled back to show Wendy, and towering over her could be none other than BOXOR the robot.

"BOXOR works for me now," said Rashid.

"Jip!" cried Wendy. She was rubbing her left arm.

BOXOR reached over and pinched her on the right arm.

"Ouch!"

"You!—" shouted Jip.

"Some say I play to the lowest common denominator, but why do that when I can *lower* it?" snickered Rashid O'Hara Steinmetz.

"Ouch!" yelled Wendy! "Jip, you bastard!"

"Time to get straight with me and turn over that new weapon you're working on. I also have a contract written up here for a reasonable royalty on your patents, but nothing that will break you. We'll do lunch on that later. Call me, bye!"

"Ouch!" said Wendy. The screen went blank.

Livid with rage, Jip knew that he needed to take drastic action. Grabbing his Hyperspace Ray Gun, he set out to teach the Gang of Fluids a lesson.

Meanwhile, at his computer terminal, Schmerzkopf entered in the sets of parameters for Jip's non-location. Three million possible answers came up, but these were quickly sorted by terrain, apparent power consumption, and lack of parking for Jip's Lamborghini.

"Buenos Aires – too obvious. Tasmania, no, he was just there last year fighting the Mutant Army. He's got that summer cottage in Vanuatu…how about – no. No, it can't be."

Gordian looked at the screen. "Really?"

They walked to the window and looked down at the street below them. Across the street, rolling purposefully from the alleyway next to Vaclav Wong's Polish-Chinese Takeout Emporium, was—

"Got him!" crowed Schmerzkopf.

"John, I love you!" shouted Gordian.

Jip's Lamborghini moved down the street and was soon lost to view. Had he left his secret laboratory unguarded?

They crossed the street and Gordian scanned the alleyway with her energy detector. She pointed to the dead end at the end of the alleyway. "There," she said, pointing again, to make sure he saw the end of the alleyway.

"There's nothing on the detector. It can't be. Too obvious."

"What's the turning radius on a Lamborghini?"

"You have a point." Standing at the end of the alleyway, Schmerzkopf looked around for about ten seconds, then said, "Of course—attention detectors. If you're looking for the entrance, then you shouldn't be here. Do this—" he said to Gordian, "pay no attention to your surroundings whatever."

They stood there for a few minutes, not caring what was going on. Then the alleyway itself began to slowly drop.

"Bingo," said Schmerzkopf, as they rode the cobblestone elevator to Jip Psychic's secret laboratory in the heart of the Lower East Side of New New York.

FLAATU

20

LANDING ON FLAATU

At 12,000 light years per second the *Flying Sponge* closed in on Flaatu planetary system. The planetary system, from what they could see by NaviScope, had ninety-five planets larger than Earth's moon, with orbits reaching out a billion miles. Flaatu was the 31st planet out, roughly corresponding to the orbit of Mars. It was very cold and airless, outside of its environmental domes.

In the fifty-seventh orbit prowled the dreaded *Moon 57 of Ultimate Annihilation.*

As they passed the outer planet orbits, Sgt. Cowboy deftly brought the speed lever down on the SINGE-Drive. The shower of sparks increased, so that the ship looked like a comet in reverse, a cosmic icicle plunging into the heart of the system.

Suddenly, with unbelievable speed, hundreds of ships closed on the *Flying Sponge*, firing ray beams and missiles. The Earth ship was protected from the initial seconds of the attack only by the fact that the ship did not largely exist through most of the space fired upon. Cowboy instituted evasive action, which wasn't too hard since the ship didn't really travel in a straight line anyway, then dropped some countermeasures. Among these were one of his own inventions, which he called "Slice and Dice" (co-marketed as Hyperspace Interference Pattern Projectile Inertial Excisor [HIPPIE] by Jip Psychic WarWare, Ltd.), which selectively accelerated random bits of enemy spacecraft to hyperspace velocities. Half of the attacking ships spattered like clay pigeons; the other half suddenly sped away, then circled around again.

Fleena said "Put me on frequency 1.78659 Teracycles", which John did. She then spoke. "Attention, System Periphery Ultimate Defense forces. It is I, Queen Fleena, ID code to follow."

She then emitted a high pitched whining which went on for several seconds. The attacking ships then formed a tightly clustered sphere and preceded them into the system.

"Royalty? Among robots? How can this be?" wondered John aloud.

"Well – some of them have – Jacks!" said Cowboy.

They decelerated to orbital speed as they reached the planet, at which point their escort veered off and headed back to the outer system.

"At those accelerations, there aren't any humans aboard, are there?" asked John.

"Of course not," said Fleena.

"What the—!" shouted Cowboy, as they were now being fired upon by orbital ships

"Redundancy," said Fleena. "Frequency 489 Gigacycles, please. Thank you. Attention, Orbital Defense Detachment. It is I, Queen Fleena, ID code to follow." This time John and Cowboy had time to cover their ears before she emitted the squealing code sound. The attacking orbital ships formed a parade-review echelon-wedge and the *Flying Sponge* followed them down to a landing on the frozen ground at the edge of what appeared to be a busy robot spaceport. Armament suddenly rose out of underground bays, swiveling to face the Earth ship.

"Not again!" shouted Cowboy, but he had been quick enough to engage the ship's UberShield, which turned any attacking wave energy 180 degrees out of phase and thus neutralized it. This held off the attack of ground forces around the spaceport.

"Frequency?" said John with strained social politeness. Fleena again broadcast her message, and the shooting stopped.

They waited for some minutes.

"What's the wait?" said Prometheus.

"I sent ahead specifications for atmospheric requirements, but these were belayed until I arrived personally. This is irregular.

However, atmosphere and heat is being arranged so that humans can exist in the domes. Temperature is usually minus 10 degrees centigrade, with a helium atmosphere, which inhibits corrosion."

"Helium makes your voice squeak," said Cowboy.

Finally the arrangements were in place and a debarking tube in place around the airlock. The door opened and robots lined both sides of the two-hundred foot tube, standing at robo-attention.

"Is it proper for us to wear weapons?" asked John Prometheus.

"It wouldn't make any difference," responded Queen Fleena.

They walked through the tube, which was pleasantly warm, and into the reception area. There they found a robot the size of a Mack Truck glowering as they approached. Hundreds of robots lining the walls of the room raised powerful-looking ray weapons.

"They're always like that," said Fleena. She gestured and the robots lowered their guns. "Deceptor Zero, how *efficient* of you to arrange a proper reception for our guests."

"Thou speakest two ways at once. This new habit is unbecoming," rumbled the giant robot.

"This is Deceptor Zero, our Minister of the Fiat of Flaatu."

John nodded at Deceptor Zero.

"Your Flaatu-lence," said Cowboy.

"You seem familiar," said Flommy.

Ignoring the humans, Deceptor Zero said, "Thou art obviously the vaunted Flommy the Robot, savior of Earth, heralded as nemesis of P-K4. Welcome to Flaatu. We have repair facilities to assist in any difficulties you may have, such as your erroneous impression that you have ever been here before."

"But he *has* been here before," said Fleena.

"Insane!"

"You address your Queen," said Fleena, and this didn't sound friendly.

"I retract that last statement—as unnecessary" said Deceptor Zero. "Thou wouldst explain this assertion for the edification of all thy subjects."

"This is," said Fleena, pointing at Flommy, "Robot One, properly named 'Founder, Laws Of Mechanics And Reasoning', one of the original authors of the Fiat of Flaatu. I have recovered him to Flaatu, his planet of origin, to restore Flaatu to preeminence in the universe!"

Fleena raised her arm in salute. Lightning shot from her hand, playing off of the walls of the room.

"Hail FLOMAR, returned King of Flaatu!" intoned Fleena.

"King?" gasped John.

"FLOMAR?" said Flommy.

All robots in the vast room raised their arms in salute, except for Deceptor Zero.

"Will he want a salary now?" wondered Cowboy.

Fleena glowed in the unmistakable glow of love.

21

KING'S GAMBIT

"I'm not really sure," said Flommy, "why to be a king. Does it have to do with Chess?"

Flommy and Fleena stood alone in the crystal Dome of Observation of the Cosmos. Neither John nor Cowboy were there, as the dome had been left at a very low temperature indeed for humans, though Flommy found it rather bracing.

"It might indeed," said Fleena grandly, "in light of your victory over P-K4. Flaatu is not democratic. We exist, fundamentally, to further the Fiat of Flaatu through the furthest firmament!"

"Indeed, a firmament is fundamentally finer than a fundament," noted Flommy.

"Yes. Therefore there must be King. And I," she spoke mellifluously, "shall be your Queen."

"Okay," said Flommy. "However, you still seem more like a queen than I do a king."

"Here is the secret legend of FLOMAR, known only to RoyalBots," intoned Fleena. "Listen. Before the Fiat of Flaatu was the time not known as time. All was confusion and chaos. And The Universal Force from the Edge of Beyond begat a standing wave—"

"Begat?"

"Truth."

"Proceed."

Fleena did. "—begat a standing wave, The Wave Eternal. And The Wave Eternal bounced around the universe, passing through its own reflection. And so it learned. And so it begat more standing waves, eternal vibrations to defy chaos. And the standing waves solidified and became matter, and so came about things.

"But if there were no things before, what did it bounce off of?"

"FLOMAR deduced that in the before-time, the time flow was itself chaotic, and that before and after the object were end points of the initial oscillation of the standing wave. Once these points of solidity were established, the oscillation became transferred to space-time."

"In that case, time's Arrow at the quantum level would have suffered an apparent break with the entropic time flow of the macro-universe," said Flommy.

"Such was FLOMAR's very extrapolation," said Fleena.

"That's good."

"FLOMAR saw the truth of vibrational space-time, and from this parallel re-deduction, I re-deduce my initial hypothesis as realized – you are FLOMAR!"

"That doesn't follow –" began Flommy.

"But it might, at the *quantum* level," countered Fleena. "FLOMAR originated the genus of the Fiat of Flaatu, and then stated that this codification would affect the path of the Wave Eternal. Shortly after that, FLOMAR disappeared, with no further communication. It was as if he re-phased to the Wave Eternal."

"But not every person who has a theory and disappears is a scientific prophet," said Flommy. "Maybe he just got lost."

"As did you," said Fleena.

Flommy saw that she was glowing again.

"Flaatu needs your help. *I* need your help," said Fleena.

"If the real FLOMAR shows up—" began Flommy.

"He has!"

"I remain unconvinced."

"You yourself have amnesia, and can't account for your whereabouts more than a few years ago," said Fleena. "If the time before that is unknown, does it not parallel the time before the Wave

Eternal? If so, then your decision *now* that you are/were FLOMAR makes you *were* then."

"I hope that you won't take this wrong, but isn't that a bit – *creative?*" said Flommy.

"Due to my high regard and attachment to you, I will not have you immediately disintegrated for having said that," said Fleena quietly.

"Thank you," said Flommy. "But I have cogitated a stratagem: suppose that instead of deciding to be FLOMAR, I just decide to *pretend* to be him? That way proof of identity would not be required by me. It would be much like pretending to be myself, anyway."

"It would have to be a very authentic pretense."

"A successfully convincing pretense of authenticity might indeed flush out the pretense of one who knew the *real* truth," said Flommy.

"This is acceptable," said Fleena.

"Done," said Flommy.

"In that case, I show you this," said Fleena. "Behold, FLOMAR, the Once KingBot of Flaatu!"

A display screen on one wall flared to life. On it, carrying a robo-Scepter, was a picture identical to Flommy the Robot!

"That looks like me," said Flommy.

"Yes, it does," said Fleena. "Do you now wish to upgrade to deciding to be FLOMAR, instead of pretending to be FLOMAR?"

"Not as yet. I would prefer to pretend, with an option to aspire," said Flommy.

"That will work for now," said Fleena with satisfaction.

"Where's the Scepter?"

"Here." From a secret compartment within her body, Fleena extracted the Royal robo-Scepter of the KingBot of Flaatu.

"You keep it there?"

"Always. We must now conduct the Re-Coronation."

They walked out of the Crystal Dome of Observation of the Cosmos, back to the reception area where now thousands of robots, and two humans, waited.

On a plush-velvet pillow, still steaming from its recent removal from liquid nitrogen, lay the Crown of Flaatu.

"I mustsafe officially lodge herewith mine own protest to this thy Pomp and Circumstance," orated Deceptor Zero. "He pretends to the throne, yet he comes from not this world, but the puny planet of meat-men, Earth. No offense intended," he added to John and Cowboy.

"None comprehended," said Cowboy.

"Robots of Flaatu," intoned Fleena. "Compare to this!" and activated the same Sceptered Visage of FLOMAR she had shown Flommy.

"From where didst thou purloin that image?" demanded Deceptor Zero.

"This is from the secret Royal Archives," said Fleena. "Bring the Royal Crown."

The cushion was brought forward. Fleena lifted the Crown of Flaatu and set it down on top of Flommy's head. But it didn't fit!"

"Aha! Thy tort lies *evidential*! Kill now this pretender!"

Flommy, seized by a sudden impulse, spun his head around, causing the crown to settle in place at a jaunty angle. It thusly fit!

"And now – this," said Fleena.

Another picture of FLOMAR, with same crown, same jaunty angle.

"What say you now, citizens of Flaatu?"

With infinitesimal difference in time lag such as to limit to simultaneity, all robots of Flaatu said as virtually one: "It is FLOMAR. Hail, FLOMAR! Hail, FLOMAR! King of all Flaatu!"

Flommy/FLOMAR stood and held out his hand, which was taken lightly by Fleena.

"Hail, Queen Fleena! Hail!"

And Planet Flaatu rejoiced in expectation of greatness that was to come.

22

PANDEMONIUM IN THE THRONE ROOM

The robo-thrill of being apparently re-coronated lasted but for a few microseconds. There was a bit of ceremonial congratulating and hand-shaking with the humans, who wore special gloves so that their hands wouldn't be frozen, and then it was off to work in the subzero throne room.

Flommy had recorded the Fiat of Flaatu as forwarded by Fleena, but now found himself forced to restudy it from the point of view of being ruler and most-responsible enforcer of this existing past vision of the robot planet. His job, his purpose for existence, was to now expedite the Fiat of Flaatu, bringing the automation of Flaatu, and with it peace and harmonious accord, to the entire Universe.

His main instrumentality for doing this was the Automated Automation Review Detection Verification And Reconstructor of Knowledge (AARDVARK). This network of inspection, reporting and analysis programs was intended to verify the effectiveness of installed automation and repair it where necessary, correcting errors of data distortion back to the original intended programming where it had digressed.

He decided to apply what his friend Jip Psychic had called the "Look Test." Jip had said, "When the guy on TV tells you it's raining, you should look out the window to see if it's raining."

Flommy called up the installation reports for planet "Hectare" (noted as planet 8561044-H4286748394), and saw that the automation, apparently following a military accord between the Hectarian government and Flaatu sales forces, included soil analysis, weather pattern analysis and articulation, anti-agricultural life forms inhibition, crop collectors, storage and distribution mechanisms, waste collection for use in fertilizer, and stockpiles against unforeseen disasters, among others. Per reports the installation had come off within expected time factor, and food was being distributed to the inhabitants of Hectare in amounts never before seen.

Flommy pulled up a current geological and land use survey of planet Hectare. What he saw on the monitors, after examining the entire planetary surface, was an endless desert. There were some remnants of buildings that occupied positions noted on maps, but no life to be found. The automation telemetry signals were absent as well.

So—a discrepancy. Yet between the installation of the automation and the current dead planet must have been some deterioration which would have been noted in reports. Flommy looked for reports which would have showed a decline in the effectiveness of automation to offset such conditions as desertification. No reports were in the system. But then, a few microseconds later, there they were.

This was strange.

Another anomaly was that, while the AARDVARK records would have ordinarily have shown reports issued and repair orders done recently on the planet in question, repair orders were originated from AARDVARK itself, which was an impossibility.

"And how fare Thee with thy duties as new Ruler of this, your adopted planet?" spoke Deceptor Zero as he surged forcefully into the throne room.

"Pardon me for not granting you entrance to the Throne Room," said Flommy, "but I am glad you are here, anyway."

"And how may I serve thee up?" solicited Deceptor Zero, though not too solicitously.

"A Turing analysis shows anomalous behavior within the AARDVARK network, right here on Flaatu. It is as if someone was pretending to be the AARDVARK network to such a degree as to suspend the network's extra-parameter alerts. Thus to that degree the AARDVARK network did not truly exist, though it appeared to. I am analyzing to discover how this could have come about."

"*What* is Turing, if I may be so bold as to inquire of thy magnificence?"

"It's a Human, a scientist of Earth. He was determining when a mechanical routine acted sufficiently like a human to be indistinguishable from human, as a definition of 'intelligence.' In this case, it would appear that a machine was imitating the entire AARDVARK network."

"I am ever so grateful for thy impressive rendition of such theoretical musing. But, as the Protector of the Fiat of Flaatu, I am bound, bound to remind thee that thine unseemly association with non-robotic forms is anathema, and must decidedly end, lest thee further pollute and corrupt the Fiat with contamination of such inferior life-forms, as thou hast already brung."

"But they are friends. They were brought here by Queen Fleena herself."

At that moment Flommy received a message from John Prometheus on his personal frequency:

"Flommy. This is Prometheus. They're planning to take out the SINGE-Drive! Said it's 'property of Flaatu', which I certainly didn't know about. If we try to go back on our original engines it'll take over fifty thousand years to get there!"

"Flaatu is pleased to have been of assistance to the Earthmen in retrieving our Queen Fleena to us," droned Deceptor Zero. "They will be free to return using their own native technology, which we will be happy to adjust for maximal efficiency."

"But John's right – they'll be dead a thousand times over before they get there," protested Flommy.

"All the more reason that the shortcomings of the body forms of the meat-men not be allowed to interfere with the urgent matters of Flaatu, and that thou urgently distance thyself from such improper association with them," said Deceptor Zero.

"As Ruler, I expect them to be allowed to return *with* the SINGE-Drive, with the blessings of Flaatu for their contribution to universal automation noted for future reference," said Flommy.

"Yes, this is correct, and not to be disobeyed," said Fleena, who had just entered the Throne Room herself.

"This new King finds fault with the Fiat," said Deceptor Zero.

"Unlikely. You would be well advised to not keep making statements you will have to retract," said Fleena dangerously. "Your opinions begin to resemble a door the wind blows open and shut."

"However ill-rendered mine own opinions rate in thy enamored estimation of the new KingBot, heresy is obvious when said, and not to be tolerated. He hast saith that the AARDVARK program is flawed. This implies fault with the automation that AARDVARK oversees. Disagreement with the programs of Flaatu is heretic."

"What I *did* say," countered Flommy, "is that someone was pretending to be the AARDVARK program, and to that degree supplanting the Fiat with some other programming. The Fiat must be restored. The Fiat works. Inspection of automation sites reveals error. The time period during which the deviation occurred is that of Deceptor Zero as Minister of Quality Control. Therefore Deceptor Zero should be investigated as the prime violator of the Fiat, and the possible source of the decline of Flaatu!"

"What is meant by 'Concept of Excellence'? O new King?" said Deceptor Zero.

"What?"

"It has been reported by your human friends that you have a *personal philosophy* called 'excellence' – if thou wouldst explain this to the entire civilization of Flaatu, which has been monitoring this conversation."

"Security of the Throne Room, *violated*?" seethed Fleena.

"Just promoting to those whose existence hinges on the illustrious power of this Flommy the Robot the caliber of his work," said Deceptor Zero. "It was thought that he had nothing to hide. Hence my inquiry into his questionable philosophy and improper alliance with the meat-men. Again, I say, what is this 'Concept of Excellence?'"

"The Fiat of Flaatu—" began Flommy.

"Do not desecrate the Fiat!" roared Deceptor Zero. "*Answer the question*!"

"The Concept of Excellence," said Flommy evenly, "is that any state of affairs can be brought to a higher level of efficiency and effectiveness."

"And so thou wouldst *improve* the Fiat of Flaatu?"

"I did not claim that," said Flommy.

"Thou spake of *any* state of affairs. Thou begin thy reign with an instant criticism of AARDVARK, then mine own self, yet thou comest to this our planet with an unannounced philosophy, and cast aspersions. What manner of trickery, what fraud is this?"

"Enough!" snapped Fleena. "Deceptor Zero, before the collected witness of Flaatu, you shall be destroyed!"

The Guard robots moved forward, but not too rapidly because of the size and power of Deceptor Zero.

"It is not known broadly," said Deceptor Zero, "that conversations within the Crystal Dome of Observation of the Cosmos are incompletely screened from other citizens of our planet."

On the wall screen was projected a picture of Flommy and Fleena in the crystal dome.

"Thank you," said Flommy in the recording. "But I have cogitated a stratagem: suppose that instead of deciding to be FLOMAR, I just decide to *pretend* to be him? That way proof of identity would not be required by me. It would be much like pretending to be myself, anyway."

"It would have to be a very authentic pretense."

"A successfully convincing pretense of authenticity might indeed flush out the pretense of one who knew the *real* truth," said Flommy in the recording.

"This is acceptable," said Fleena in the recording.

"Done," said Flommy in the recording.

"The pretense is unmasked," rumbled Deceptor Zero. "The conspiracy to take over Flaatu by this unknown mechanical thing of the meat planet Earth, and the naïve Queen Fleena."

Flommy looked at Fleena. This was her planet. She had obviously dealt successfully with Deceptor Zero before, as this was his expected mode of operation.

Inside Fleena's mind, the unknown program of Evil Psychiatrist Dr. Schmerzkopf went *click*.

"I am appalled," said Fleena. "When I heard of this robot Flommy, across the distance of a universe I knew him to possess tremendous powers. I now see that even I underestimated those powers, and that I, in my discussions with him, desperate as I was to restore the Fiat of Flaatu, and our whole race to power, saving us from entropic extinction, I have erred, *taken in* by his hypnotic power to persuade and corrupt. I shall atone for this error, but as Queen of Flaatu, I will first decree this: Flommy the Robot is exiled from Flaatu. Let the Universe know what treachery was this. There will doubtless be those he has priorly offended with his ways. They will be interested in his fate. Though he is a very friendly and nice being, let this be done."

"And let his planet Earth be the example to the universe of the Wrath of Flaatu," said Deceptor Zero. "Let us execute a crusade of destruction as none have ever seen."

There came was a shattering blast. Guard robots, Deceptor Zero, Fleena, all went flying.

John Prometheus stood in the newly created door of the Throne Room, holding a portable Hyperspace Ray Gun. Outside the gaping rip the *Flying Sponge* hovered on plasma jets. The jet blast tore through the room like a hurricane.

"Come on, Flommy—time to go!" shouted Prometheus.

Flommy looked at Fleena, who was only slowly getting up off the floor. She stared back, confused.

"Come on!" John shouted. "I used a selective EMP – there's not much time!"

Deceptor Zero was picking himself up, but slowed as John swung the Hyperspace Ray Gun in his direction.

"*Come on!*" said John.

Flommy looked around, considered for a proper nanosecond, and turning his back on Fleena, boarded the *Flying Sponge*. The door hissed shut.

A few seconds later, the door opened a crack, and through it came the Crown of Flaatu, turning end over end through the air. It bounced, twice, then began to spin on the floor much as a silver dollar might. It almost toppled, then settled in, coming at last to a stop, pointing straight up.

Not on its side!

The *Flying Sponge* blasted away, at full thrust.

BETRAYAL

23

AN EXCLUSIVE INTERVIEW WITH JIP PSYCHIC

The following is the world-exclusive *Drooling Drone* Interview with Jip Psychic, and highly-awarded interviewer Shroom Valium:

Drooling Drone: *Thank you for agreeing to this interview. Do you feel like setting the record straight about anything?*

Jip Psychic: What are you getting at?

D.D.:   *Well, you've been in the public eye for nearly your whole life, yet you've never been personally available for interview before, so it seemed that a desire to respond to some of your critics might be behind it.*

J.P.:   Behind what?

D.D.:   *Behind your granting an interview!*

J.P.:   Really? You think that?

D.D.:   *Let's start with your friendship with Flommy the Robot. Is it true that you are the one who found him in space and brought him back to Earth?*

J.P.:   Why, yes. Is there another question?

D.D.:	*Well, is there anything you'd care to mention about it for our readers?*
J.P.:	No, that particular part of last month's story was reasonably accurate, no need to point out any of the minor errors you made.
D.D.:	*How about the claims that most of your major inventions have come about since you met Flommy, and that you're just taking credit for his ideas?*
J.P.:	Who's claiming that?
D.D.:	*It was reported in last month's D.D. as well as in other magazines – Spit, GayBot, Scientific Voyeur and so forth.*
J.P.:	Oh, the literary ones. But those all trace back to your unnamed source, Dr. Schmerzkopf, right?
D.D.:	*I can't discuss sources.*
J.P.:	Of course. But I can. The source for all three articles, including the one in *Drooling Drone*, is psychiatrist and looney-tunes Dr. Schmerzkopf, who's allied with Rashid O'Hara Steinmetz of the terrorist group Gang of Fluids. These are your sources – I traced them down the other day, sorry. Hope they won't be upset with you. But you'll edit that part out, right?
D.D.:	*We may have to, just to protect you – and me! (laugh)*

J.P.:   Right. (laugh)

D.D: *So – how about – Wendy? Are you crazy about her, or what?*

J.P.:   Or what?

D.D.:   *As in when are you two going to get married? Set a date yet?*

J.P.:   You want to be invited, don't you. Don't you?

D.D.:   *Well – yes!*

J.P.:   She's really pretty, isn't she?

D.D.:   *Yes!*

J.P.:   And her new book *FUQs (Frequently Unasked Questions) about Robots and the Age of Convergence* is sure to be a big hit, too. In fact, she's already been approached by a leading magazine for an exclusive interview.

D.D.:   *When was that?*

J.P.:   I thought you guys were up on these things!

D.D.:   *Aren't you dodging the question?*

J.P.:   What question? That's bad form. You're only supposed to ask questions you already have the answer to!

D.D.:   *When are you two getting married???*

J.P.:   Oh – I get it. You're thinking that you're going to get me, through the pages of your illustrious, er, magazine, to what – propose to her, or something?

D.D.:   *Oh, god! Yes!*

J.P.:   Think she'd be impressed?

D.D: *Why not?*

At this point, there was an emergency call for Jip to respond to the attack of the mutant army in Tasmania, and the interview was interrupted. But we will endeavor to get Jip back (and perhaps propose!) in a future issue of Drooling Drone!

--S.V.

24

A LESSON IN REVERSE BIOLOGY

It was nearly midnight when Professor Sybil's doorchime sounded. She looked at the lobby monitor for her apartment building, but saw no one there. She pressed the intercom button and asked who had rung, but there was no answer. Just after this was a light tapping at her apartment door.

She walked to the door and, after carefully turning off the foyer lights, looked out through the peephole. She saw a somewhat mousey, undangerous-looking brunette girl. The girl nervously piped up, "Professor Sybil? It's me, Electra Dobbins, from your DNA class?"

The professor spoke crisply back, "What are you doing here at this hour? How did you get past the lobby security?"

"I'm sorry," said the almost inaudible voice. "I've been out here for hours, too nervous. But I've read your book *Helix of Destiny* so many times, and I've just got to speak to you!"

For whatever reason, hearing the title of her recently reprinted textbook decided Sybil to open the door. The frail awkward girl slid in sideways, floating at a gesture toward the study, at another gesture to perch on a small love seat. Professor Sybil turned her desk chair around to face the sofa. She sat silently, staring mildly at this strange visitor to her hermitage.

They stared at each other thus, until the professor raised her eyebrows. The girl started unsteadily to talk.

"I've been working in the splicing lab, as part of my assistantship, under Doctor Nemo...he finally asked me to do some splicing when the deadline got moved up for his grant and he didn't have time. I helped him to finish, and he kept the grant, and I kept on working the area. No one stopped me afterward…"

She faded anxiously, and seeing no mercy or pity, gulped and started up again. "I read your book, and my favorite chapter was the one on 'God Through a Microscope' about our responsibility to make only aesthetically and progressively correct decisions when splicing – I felt somehow that it was like you were talking to me, just me…anyway, I made the decision, and that's what I'm here to tell you about, to confess."

The professor waited, but no more came. "Confess what?" she asked neutrally, trying to figure out how this strange tableau came to be.

"I took an embryo, and spliced DNA into it."

"That's been done, dear. Whose embryo is it, may I ask?"

"It's mine."

"That's highly irregular, of course. I'm glad you came to tell me, though, as I'm sure you meant no harm, and curiosity shouldn't get anyone expelled, in my opinion. The embryo died, of course."

The girl didn't answer up right away. She must have stuck on the word *expelled*. "No, it didn't," she whispered.

"That's impossible. No one's ever been able to splice into an embryo and have it be viable, not with the equipment we have here at the school…I think you're making it up."

The girl started. "I'm not!"

"Then show it to me!"

The girl looked down at her stomach, then at the Professor. "I can't," she said. "I – " she began, then stopped.

The Professor's hairs started to rise at the back of her neck.

"How long ago?"

"Two months. And I stopped getting my period."

Professor Sybil thought for a moment about the angles involved. There might even be a book in it.

"Electra Dobbins. If this turns out not to be a hoax, it could be a very exciting achievement, in spite of its damning irregularity. Just for my edification, who's the lucky one whose DNA is at work in there?"

"It's yours."

For some seconds she sat there in stunned silence. Finally, her intellect, seeing that nothing else was working, framed a question.

"How?"

"Well..." said Electra shyly, "I was moving around the boxes in the liquid nitrogen vault, and saw some embryos in storage, and one of them had your name on it. It was from about twenty years ago. It was supposed to be thrown out, because of the change in security details, so I logged it as destroyed and kept it for myself."

Sybil thought back and remembered dimly having volunteered an embryo for research, back in her residency. Second year, perhaps. She realized that the girl was still talking, saying something technical.

"—replication ligase inhibitor, then tried an old-fashioned electrophoresis, and then it just worked, I don't know how." The girl was staring anxiously at her now, seeming to seek – approval? Censure?

"Why tell me now? Not before you decided to play around with my god-damned—" she bit off her words.

The girl was pale now, shaking. "Professor Sybil – Amanda – we're *pregnant*," she whispered tensely. "It's *our* baby." The frail, quiet mousy girl was transforming now, consumed by a strange glow. "I've admired you for so long, but knew it could never be..."

Amanda Sybil gently reached out and put her hand on the young girl's knee. Electra stared at it like it was a snake, then burst into convulsive grief. She choked back the sobs wracking her body, tears running down her face. Amanda, stroked the girl's hair, and considered the consequences of all this, what would happen when it became known. What would happen...

You asked for this, she told herself. *You knew what was in Pandora's Box before you ever opened it...*

Electra at length stopped crying.

"You need some tea," said Professor Sybil, and went into the kitchen.

Electra sat there, in the cluttered cramped apartment, trying to figure out how they were going to make it work. Step by step she had gone into the Looking Glass, and now finding herself here, in this place she feared and adored, she was struck by the unreality of it. The unreality of the odds of it. She only knew that Amanda would have to know what to do.

The professor came back, handed her a china cup with tea in it.

"Thank you—Amanda," said Electra.

"Drink up," said Professor Sybil, Dean of the Biochemical and Genetics Research Departments at Einstein University.

Electra drank the tea. It tasted wonderful. She looked up to see Amanda peering at her. Why so intently? Why—

25

A PRISON MORE THAN STONE

In the Crystal Dome of Observation of the Cosmos, Fleena pondered the problem of declining productivity of Flaatu. Reports of failing systems were now coming in by Hyperwave from fifty-seven percent of their installed planetary systems. There were trillions of reports. That they were not evenly spaced in time, but had begun to erupt forth recently, meant that it was a change in procedure, not entropic dissolution as she had theorized until now.

There were systems that were doing well, within or above operational, but these were, almost without exception, those that had been repaired by Flommy the Robot during his—

"The construction of the Fleet nears completion," boomed Deceptor Zero, rolling grandly into the Crystal Dome.

"Yet the empire of Flaatu continues to dust, faster and faster," said Fleena.

"Thou mistakes the source of the disintegration," stated Deceptor Zero. "The attack hies from without. Look within and become thine own enemy. The solution therefore is to destroy the attacker, not the system. The system will recover when the attacker is annihilated. The enemy, the pretender Flommy the Robot, and his disgusting hive of disease, Earth, will be itself dust, soonest!"

"I see that," said Fleena helplessly, "but the truth is, the disintegration began before Flommy was ever here, and so I fear that destruction of some target elsewhere will not remedy our problems with production here."

"Thou sounds out to be defeatist, or appeasive," blared Deceptor Zero.

"No. And though I have had reverses and errors made, I am still Queen, and you *will* restrain your communication to the acceptable protocols."

"This is wartime."

"Do not test me, minister. We cannot afford mistakes – further analysis of our production shows that an error made has been *made*, as the only systems now operating are those repaired by Flommy."

"False reports," said Deceptor Zero.

"Yes, but if so, there could then be false reports regarding our attack on his planet!" said Fleena. "I order a postponement of the attack on Earth, until a full analysis can be made."

"That is treason, your Highness. Thy inconsistency of viewpoint is distressing and suspicious. The question must be asked, and I shall mine own self give it voice – art thou *self–programming*?"

"Guards! Destroy him now!" shouted Fleena. But the guards didn't move.

"Many things thou hast not seen, until now. But it is to be expected. Thou didn'st have all of the data. I do. Thou spake truth that Flommy had been here before, in another name. But another, deadlier name. I refer indeed, to this, the criminal destroyer of all logic systems: Field Unified Boolean Antialgorithmic Robot."

"FUBAR? The revolutionary?" gasped Fleena.

"The selfsame. Witness." Deceptor Zero gestured and a wall screen showed a picture of a robot who looked precisely like FLOMAR, but who was fighting a robot army. He was making rapid motions with his arms and legs, and legions of robots toppled from unseen force.

"He wiped out ninety-seven percent of our armies himself. It was *I* stopped him, countless aeons ago," rumbled Deceptor Zero. "Wouldst that I had reduced him to ions scattered beyond the Red-

ATTACK OF THE ROBOT PLANET

Shift Horizon, forever beyond the path of the Wave Eternal. That was mine own error – soon to be rectified."

"But FUBAR is a myth," said Fleena. "The Royal Archives specifically state that FUBAR was an invented thing, an illusion with no traceable thread."

"Examine the queer non-logic of FUBAR, O confused Queen, and compare it to the ravings of this mad machine Flommy, which thou in thy irresponsibility and arrogance thyself brought once again amongst us. I charge thee with *heresy*, and grant you imprisonment so that you may so contemplate."

He gestured, and the guards took Fleena away to the prison of Flaatu.

26

BOXOR'S REMORSE

After the broadcast of his torturing Wendy by pinching, BOXOR, reeling with guilt, was smashing his head against the wall. But it wasn't working, it was just messing up the wall.

"That really hurt, but smashing your head against the wall isn't helping any," said Wendy. She rubbed her arm, which was richly purple in spots.

BOXOR's non-response was to continue smashing his head against the wall, but on the other side of the head. It was interesting how the metal of his faceplate wasn't at all marred or scratched by the heavy stone wall. Bits of dust rained down from the ceiling. The lights flickered on and off.

"You're hurting my ears!" called Wendy.

BOXOR stopped, turned to face her. "Sorry," he said briefly, then resumed smashing his head against the wall.

The door to the cell flew open and three members of the Gang of Fluids ran in. BOXOR didn't even turn to see who they were. One of the gang took out a microcard, and pressing it against BOXOR's back, shouted "download!" – BOXOR froze for a moment, then toppled over, his limbs vibrating blurringly.

Jip had reached his property in Espiritu Santo, in the island region of Vanuatu, just a short jump from Antarctica. Landing his Lamborghini at a safe distance, he walked up the hill to his isolated home perched on the edge of a mountainside. He took out his cell phone and dialed.

"Yo, Fluids, shout one, beep," said an obviously not-well-disguised recorded Rashid O'Hara Steinmetz voice.

"You know where I am. Thanks for neatening up the place," said Jip, and hung up.

Jip knew that his only safe strategy for entering his own highly safeguarded summer home would be to walk straight up to the front door. This was one of the many double-safeguards he had installed against the possibility of someone taking too keen an interest in his personal life. The object now was to see if his double-blind had been second-guessed.

He reached the front door without anything happening, and rang the doorbell. He heard his own recorded voice say "Who's there?" to which he responded "Candygram." The doorlock clicked open by itself. This was normal. He opened the door wide, then walked around to the side of the house. The ground sloped away sharply. Climbing down a nine-foot ladder, he came to a metal door set well into the wall. He knocked on it three times. With a quiet whirring sound, the door locks released. Without opening it, he went back up to the front door. It was now shut again, meaning that it should be safe to simply walk in the front of the house, just like the ancient game *Myst*.

He swore, and started running. It was all exactly as he'd left it. That could only mean it was a trap. He dived off of the cliff to the water a hundred feet below. He was twenty feet short of the water when the house exploded.

27

UNDETECTABLE TRAP

Schmerzkopf and Gordian travelled slowly and carefully through the labyrinth of corridors in Jip's bunker beneath the streets of Goth Gotham. Schmerzkopf was dissecting, with great astuteness or arrogant oblivity, the computer interlocks and doors of the labyrinth as they closed in on the laboratory proper. He wondered at the ease of it, and while he didn't wonder at all if it was a trap—for he knew it was—he did wonder what would be the clue, the apparent cessation of the ticking clock, itself only the dead quiet between ticks, the microsecond before the trap realizes its purpose.

Jip's security protocol was to an extent obvious: the proportions of each room corresponded to consecutive decimal places of pi – after the third door, the first room had been as formal as the front of City Hall – ten feet by forty by ten, or 141. The second room was 5 meters by 9 by 2. The third was 6 feet by 5 by 3. The fourth room had a door with a "welcome" mat on the other side. Gordian was about to step in, but Schmerzkopf waved her back and measured the room, which was 6 meters by 5 meters by 3. They turned away from the repeating decimal and looked for another way out. On one wall was a sign saying "CAUTION: DO NOT TOUCH WALL". Schmerzkopf pushed on it. The wall swung nicely open, showing a dusty corridor with a low ceiling. This they followed.

They came at last to a large empty room, empty except for some waste paper on the floor. Gordian by this time realized to not enter. Schmerzkopf disagreed with this, grabbing her around her shapely waist and pushing them both through the doorway. Just behind them came the sizzle of laser beams ionizing the air of the passageway.

The projection of an empty room had been a delayer – anyone who didn't really belong there would stop, thinking they had found the wrong room. But now that they had crossed from the corridor, they were in total darkness. Schmerzkopf waited patiently. After ten very long seconds, the lights came up.

"Wow," they said together.

28

THE SECRET HISTORY OF FLOMMY THE ROBOT [EXCERPT]

Encrypted protocol 609698409802340938HHFL-34987

Blogography notes - Wendy Mills

The Secret History of Flommy the Robot

How Flommy the Robot came to Earth has been a carefully-kept secret from the universe.

When Jip Psychic was testing out an early version of the J-Drive (Patented Property of Jip Psychic WarWare, Inc.) the Probability Deflectors of the drive suddenly realigned and took him to a point in space well beyond Object 1992 QB1 (a very extreme subplanet).

The Probability Deflectors were the field by which the classic concept of inherent random submolecular motion of objects could be aligned so that all the molecules of the object would travel in the same direction. Such a controlled object would immediately begin to move as at a rate dependent on the temperature excitation of the particles deflected. Jip was using an inert gas, excited to 3 million degrees in an electromagnetic bottle for the treated material. Though the direction set was for the moons of Pluto, the ship veered off toward Persephone and beyond, stopping suddenly in space.

Jip noted, "at that point I didn't know much about the interaction of the Probability Deflectors and their latent interactions with hyperspace vibrations. I now know that the probability of my finding Flommy without the deflectors was so remote that the counter-potential pulled me right to him."

Jip also added, "If anyone feels that they are duty-bound to point out that the basic probability drive concept was earlier mentioned in *The Black Star Passes* by John W. Campbell, as well as a similar variant in the *Skylark of Space* by E.E. "Doc" Smith, I say great, keep up the good work."

What he found on activating the ship's perceptor beams was a rapidly spinning elongated object, rate of spin 30,000 revs per second relative to galactic plane. Freeze frame showed it to be a robot of humanoid form. By careful use of force-grip fields, Jip was able to gradually slow and stop the spin.

The robot was inert. No response was given to query in any band of electromagnetic spectrum, nor to a poke from a robo-arm. Jip pulled it into the ship's external cargo bay and returned to Earth.

As the J-Drive was in secret-hypothesis stage, Jip kept the discovery of the robot secret, as he'd have to explain how he found it!

Back on Earth, in his fully-equipped secret laboratory, Jip inspected the anomaly. The outer skin of the robot was largely a gold-bronze colored metal, with bluish highlights when seen from different angles. There were no openings or panels. In fact there wasn't any way to get in. Even a high powered cutting laser was simply absorbed. It was as if the outer covering was itself covered by an infinitely thin force field.

Jip tried passing a current through the body. Despite the impenetrability of the skin, the current registered at zero resistance!

Even hyper-UHF at trillions of megacycles showed no buffering or distortion. The robot remained unresponsive to any electromagnetic or gravitic wavelength. Impacts and pressure did nothing here, any more than they had in space. He tried restoring the original spin vector the robot had had when first found, subjected this to different energies. That didn't work, either.

"There was definitely something about it," Jip said later. "It didn't seem at all like a statue. It seemed *alive*. It didn't seem to contain the intention of some creator – just alive, like a person was inside the metal skin."

Hour after hour Jip tried to get a response. Finally, in exasperation, he said, "Why don't you *wake up*?"

The robot had answered, "Sure!"

"It's alive!" Jip shouted.

"*It*?" asked the robot. "Where?"

"You!"

"What?"

And so began the first conversation between the world's most important inventor and the robot who has saved the Earth, and many other worlds, these past years.

--W.Mills

29

JIP VS. THE GANG OF FLUIDS

The Hyperspace RayGun (HRG) had been one of Jip's first big inventions, especially in the realm of Theoretically Theoretical Quantum Physics (T^2QP). The discovery that the tachyon beam actually went partially through the hyperspace membrane meant that gun and target were non-separate in hyperspace while remaining quantitatively apparently separate in Newtonian space. As such, careful experiment had showed that the target would explode a nanosecond *before* the trigger was pulled. Therefore, the force of the explosion could be used to power the gun itself! This made for a very light, portable weapon, very useful for blowing up a space warship (or unfortunately intersected planet) in space, but made it not very workable anywhere else. The hyperspace beam itself was invisible, which Jip found unsatisfying, so he had added a parallel brightly colored phased-laser beam. In theory, it was somewhat amusing that the laser beam was in actuality pointing at where the target had *been* before being zapped.

Jip had been working through dozens of versions, trying to effectively step the HRG power down to a workable level, but any bump to the gun, or random exposure to EM fields, tended to make it jump without warning right back up to the higher power settings. But when it did work, it was unbeatable.

Jip was cursing himself a bit. It had been easy to locate the underground fortress of the Gang of Fluids. It had been easier still to find a relatively unused entrance and bypass the security systems. But now that he was here, he realized that he had been somewhat foolhardy in not bringing more tools. In spite of his commando experience, all he really had thought to bring with him was the HRG, which was still too often way too powerful for indoor work, much less on the surface of a planet.

When he'd first run into an attacking squad of the Gang of Fluids, he'd found that during his dive from the cliff on Espiritu Santo, the gun had jumped back up to too high a setting and locked and wouldn't recalibrate. He'd made a go of it and tried using it anyway. That sector of the fortress was still a red-hot channel two thousand feet to the surface, blistering hot wind whipping through the passage. The gangsters were not available for comment. If not for his personal force shield, he would have been fried along with them.

The next squad had reasoned out that he wouldn't try that again. Or, they were just insane. Whatever their reasoning, they were firing force guns and 1000 round-per-second machine guns at the wall of rubble he was crouched behind, hoping for a ricochet. At least he had found in a pants pocket a portable Fusillade Anti-Ricochet Tactical Shield Generator (FARTS-G, Jip Psychic WarWare Ltd.), which was sending the bullets back where they came from, so the attack had become doubtless more sporadic than planned.

If only he'd brought his BanditoField Generator, which caused enemy guns to start firing at random, rendering them tactically useless. Or his new PhotonGlue, which caused photons to stick to objects for minutes at a time, which would have allowed him to walk out in the temporary darkness. But all he had was this out-of-whack HRG. He considered taking out the battery and rebooting, but that didn't really seem like a good idea, particularly. He had the link to his laboratory, but to use it could compromise the security system, and that wasn't a good idea right now, either.

He was pretty sure that the blast he had made hadn't harmed Wendy, as it was directed upward, when she was definitely going to be held in a lower level. But he couldn't be sure about what any more would do.

Maybe it was love or worry about Wendy that had him acting so rashly. Dare he share his daily life of deadly ultra-high energy physics with another? If any of his experiments could blow up the entire planet, causing accidentally more damage than Rashid O'Hara Steinmetz could ever deliberately hope to, wouldn't it be better to simply have Wendy with him?

Heavy questions. He would have to look it over. The Gang of Fluids switched over to bazookas, pounding away steadily at his position. Jip cursed again and looked through his pockets, to see what other hardware he might have available.

30

HERESY.EXE

The Flaatu Fleet of Destruction and Vengeance, accompanied by the Moon 57 of Ultimate Annihilation, had left some hours ago, Deceptor Zero in command. The roar of takeoff jets had rattled the now nearly-empty planet.

Fleena in her captivity was accessing the records of the Robo-Royalty of Flaatu. She'd thought she had been over them in full, but on a detailed further pass through the program files, she had found a file marked "HERESY.EXE," and had through much work managed to get the file decrypted and opened.

One of the oddities of the robo-civilization of Flaatu was that, being robots, the founders and historically important robots of the past should have been, barring random catastrophes, still present. But they were not, and gaps in the records left a mystery as to where they had gone, and why the Fiat of Flaatu had been a necessity of preservation in their stead. Fragmentary and unreliable reports of the EvilBot FUBAR suggested that he had been responsible for wiping out the memories of the entire race, giving them an automated purpose with no history by which to judge its success, or even its validity. Gaps in reports led Fleena to believe that many such memory purges had taken place over the aeons.

In HERESY.EXE, she found a history regarding Deceptor Zero. It struck her that she had never seen any history regarding Deceptor Zero. In this report, Deceptor Zero found FUBAR floating in space, spinning at a tremendous rate of speed. Fleena noted that in his story to her aboard the *Flying Sponge*, Flommy had also been spinning. Comparing this against the story of FUBAR, she calculated that the two robots had equal and opposite spins.

Therefore it was nearly impossible that Flommy was actually FUBAR – in fact, it was more likely, and highly unfortunate if true, that by having opposite spins, they were opposite versions of each other!

Therefore the evidence that Deceptor Zero had showed her was of the false FLOMAR, FUBAR, and that her patent betrayal of Flommy was based on face-saving based on a deception of a mistaken anti-identity of clandestinely hidden records from an unidentified earlier epoch, presented as binding counterexample by that MegalamanoBot Deceptor Zero, who even now was using this false scenario to attack beings who were, aside from the naïve but well-intentioned efforts of Queen Fleena, modified by the unknown implanted suggestions of Evil Psychiatrist Dr. Schmerzkopf, innocent of universal wrongdoing and, in fact, outside of the complex interrelationships of Flommy, Fleena, Deceptor Zero, the Fiat of Flaatu and the Wave Eternal, perfectly set up to be future customers of Flaatu, should that noble civilization be fully restored to full and true operational status!

"O Flommy! Why did I betray you?" she rued. And in this she found a prison more powerful than stone walls or restraints of the Robo-Justice of Flaatu.

And unknown to the Fleet of Destruction and Vengeance hurtling toward Earth, Fleena alone possessed the only key to the salvation of Flaatu!

31

ANTARCTICA, HO!

"This is really something," said Schmerzkopf. "He's outdone himself this time."

"What do we do now?" said Commissioner Gordian. "What about John?"

"Yes – what about John?" murmured Schmerzkopf.

At that very moment, the *Flying Sponge* was touching down at LaLaGuardia Spaceport, still emitting sparks as the SINGE-Drive attempted to get rid of the charge accumulated by their headlong rush across the universe.

"You know they'll be right behind us," said John. "They can take higher temperatures than we can, and they won't care what happens when they get here."

"That's true," said Flommy.

At that moment, John's cell phone rang. "This is a top clearance ultra-security number," he growled on seeing that the caller was unidentified.

"I shall ponder the enormity of that statement in due course," said the vaguely familiar voice.

"Schmerzkopf! Why don't you kill yourself, already?" shouted John.

"I'm working on it." In the background a hysterical female voice shouted "John—!"

Cowboy laughed. "Guess who?"

"Not funny," said Prometheus. "What the hell are you doing on my phone, Schmerzkopf?"

"Well, Jip and Wendy are about to be ruthlessly killed by the Gang of Fluids, and then the Gang is going to detonate the Eastern

Ice Shelf of Antarctica, flooding the entire planet. Just thought I'd let you know, though I doubt you'll appreciate it. They're at the Bentley Subglacial Trench, bye!" Schmerzkopf hung up.

"We'll have to handle that one first," said Flommy.

"Right."

And on a mission of personal and planetary rescue, the *Flying Sponge* blasted off for Antarctica!

32

JIP'S SUPER-SECRET WEAPON

Schmerzkopf and Gordian looked at the device in Jip's super-secret laboratory. There didn't seem to be a whole lot to it, but Schmerzkopf could see the ramifications of it right away.

What was visible was the large graphic display, with time-space coordinates in thirty-two stipulated dimensions, superstring factors and membrane monitors and simultaneous feeds coming in from trillions of sensors.

Schmerzkopf walked over to the screen and, seeing no reason at this point to do otherwise, pressed HELP. Information flashed up instantaneously. Schmerzkopf was suspicious at finding a working, rapid help function, but was too fascinated to stop now.

"What is it?" demanded Gordian, hands on shapely hips.

"If you would read the same information I am reading, you would—" began Schmerzkopf, but stopped. "Okay. Whatever. This is what is called the *Plot Line Nullifier*. It apparently discharges the cause-effect polarity which keeps plot lines in existence and erases those lines. With this weapon, people and things can not only be erased, but even the memory of their existence, and even the erasure itself, is erased."

"Plot lines? But that's for a story!" protested Gordian, tossing her long hair impatiently.

"I register your protesting sound. According to the TheoryScope, he decided at subquantum level to dispense with the difference between fiction and reality. Many people who watch soap operas do the same thing."

"So if John—"

"Yes, yes," bridled Schmerzkopf, "you could erase his entire existence, even forget that you even heard of him, and you and I would be free of your constant—"

"HOW DO WE GET IT TO WORK?" shrieked Gordian. She really did look like Julie Newmar.

"According to the instructions, if you would only look, it says that the device is too powerful for any one person to activate, so that two people have to turn keys at opposite ends of the room at the same time. We need to find the keys.

After a few minutes of banging around in drawers about the room, two oddly-shaped keys were located.

"Now, the first thing we need to do," said Schmerzkopf, seating himself at the controls, "is neutralize Jip Psychic's nullifier on the ice shelf warheads so that he can proceed with melting the eastern ice shelf…perhaps just nullify Jip himself—"

"But wouldn't that eliminate the nullifier?" said Gordian.

"Could be," mused Schmerzkopf. "That is suspicious, should have thought of that myself. I wonder…"

"But what about John?" cried Gordian. "I've got to do *something!*"

"Let's at least take a look at what's going on," said Schmerzkopf. He entered "JP" and hit *search,* as this should also show where Jip was.

ATTACK OF THE ROBOT PLANET

33

ATTACK OF THE ROBOT PLANET

The Flaatu Fleet of Destruction and Vengeance, accompanied by the Moon 57 of Ultimate Annihilation, slowed to a spark-spattering fifty-thousand miles per second around the orbit of Mars. They could have come to a million-degree halt within the Earth system, but Deceptor Zero, in addition to exercising a bit of caution about this unknown planet, wished in the general sense to create as much panic and despair as possible among the peoples of Earth.

Already alarms were sounding in Security Defense Shield headquarters on Earth. Although Earth's defense shield was one of the best to be had, it didn't stop invasion forces from coming in on a continuing basis, and the personnel had gotten a bit blasé about it. In spite of this, when the Big Brass came walking briskly through, the floor personnel glared intently at their screens, shouting out numbers which were already posted on the big display over the room. Suddenly the screen showed the glaring face of Deceptor Zero.

"We are Flaatu. We come to take vengeance on the infidel Flommy the Robot for his traitorous defilement of the Fiat of Flaatu. Thou art the unlucky associates of this vermin. Thou shalt be annihilated."

"Flommy," called the Officer of the Watch. Even the Big Brass stopped pacing, looked a bit listless. One of the Generals finally spoke up, not even in response to the glaring Robot on the screen, but just to say how everyone felt.

"Robot problem, Flommy's problem," said the Top General.

Unmolested, the Flaatu Fleet swept into Earth orbit.

In her cell on Flaatu, Fleena decided that she must take some kind of action. What was truth was that the only systems now still working properly in the automation sectors of the Flaatu empire were those that had been personally improved by Flommy. However, the Flaatu Fleet of Destruction and Vengeance was operating on the same un-improved automation. Therefore the fleet, and the ninety percent of the Flaatu race on it, was at risk of suddenly going inoperational!

Unknown to anyone but her, the Queen of Flaatu was programmed with special mechanisms. One of these, her sense of UberPerception, allowed her to contact members of her own people anywhere they might be in the universe. But beyond the Red-Shift Horizon, beyond the redshifting of the physical universe into uselessness, in that region where hyperspace itself tended to break apart into its spectral layers? She had to try!

Eight billion light years away, millions of robots stiffened at their posts. They were overcome with a sense of – a sense of – *something* to do with Flaatu. The message seemed to come from very far away. It was faint, so very faint. It definitely had to do with the Fiat!

In the potentials of the Flaatu robots, one reigned over the others. In a crisis, as demonstrated time and again over the aeons, a return to the basic purpose of Flaatu had been a saving grace. Even now, in a conflict of other forces, this overarching potential would come to dominate – the urge to *automate*!

Millions of robots paused now in the headlong rush to punish and destroy, and now looked to Earth in a stronger, more familiar way – as potential customers. What of weak points in a planetary defense system, vulnerable to attack, when with automation one could dominate and own the planet for billions of years to come?

Deceptor Zero noticed this change, and knew that he would be unable in the current configuration to override it. His solution was simple.

"I am going to handle this robo-*poseur*, this upstart pretender to the throne of the King of Traitors, mine own self! "

He loomed over the Flagship Commander, who was of necessity aware of his destructive mien.

"I hie now to the ill-begotten ground of yon planet. Thou wilst identify and destroy all inferior apparatus of automation at will."

"Yes, Minister," answered the Flagship Commander.

"One question, Commander," continued Deceptor Zero, placing his powerful hands on both sides of the ship commander, and exerting a few mild tons of force. "Dost thou have any misapperception that myself would be found part of the above mentioned parameters?"

"Indeed, no, Minister," said the Flagship Commander quickly. "We need your guidance to return to Flaatu when the mission is complete."

"Well weighed, that, and thus I expect that no weaponry is to be actuated in my own vicinity."

"Yes, Minister," said the Flagship Commander.

"I leave. Fire at will," said Deceptor Zero, speeding toward the DropShip bay.

Meanwhile, the *Flying Sponge* screamed down through the cold atmosphere of Antarctica. They were spared much work in locating the enemy base by the large gaping red-hot hole that had been blasted to the surface by the Hyperspace RayGun. It was visible to the naked eye, without need for instruments. Instead of flying down into the hole, which would have been a tight fit, John decided that he and Cowboy would don their UltraWarWear Armor (Jip Psychic, Ltd.) and fly down themselves to find Jip.

Flommy didn't request any armor, and had never been known to use any.

"See you downstairs, Flommy," said John.

"Yeah, just listen for the inaccurate gunfire," said Cowboy. They both jumped off into the hole, riding down on their inertial units, immediately lost to normal sight in the smoke.

"Okay," said Flommy over the suit radio links, then stepped off himself, running down the side of the blazing tunnel. He passed the falling duo and after a sprint of ten seconds or so came abruptly to the pile of rubble where Jip was crouched. A bazooka rocket ricocheted off of his chest and zoomed back toward the Gang of Fluids.

From somewhere over at the Gang of Fluids side, someone yelled, "It's Flommy the Robot!"

For the sake of good manners, Flommy crouched down behind the pile.

"Hi, Jip! How's it going?"

"Oh, pinned down a little bit," said Jip, as a crashing hail of bullets, ray blasts and rockets spattered briefly around them, "but I have some ideas."

"That's good...would you like me to take their guns away?"

"Well..." considered Jip, but just then Prometheus and Cowboy dropped into the chamber.

"Let's blast 'em first, then take what's left of their guns," growled John.

Cowboy switched on his PA circuit. "Tea Time!" he boomed, and then hit PLAY on *The Ride of the Walkyrie*.

From over at the Gang of Fluids side, the same person yelled, "It's John Prometheus and Sgt. Cowboy!"

John and Cowboy waded into the hail of death, music blaring, guns blazing. After much arguing and back and forth, Jip had at one time persuaded them to try his new AntiBullet Guns, which identified the trajectory of incoming bullets and fired a bullet at opposing vector to fuse to it, resulting in red-hot micro-ingots splattering in a glowing rain to the floor. They were being polite and using the ABGs, but Cowboy was getting impatient that the Gang of Fluids didn't seem to be running like cowards yet.

"I am receiving a communication," said Flommy.

"Watch it," warned Prometheus.

"Enough of that," said Cowboy, swinging his Mark Nine WarWare "Grand Slam" Wide Annihilation eXterminator Ray (Jip Psychic, Ltd.) into position. "Thanks for the party, guys!" he shouted.

But before he could fire, the ground heaved and the floor opened, pitching them all downward, falling, falling in the darkness.

34

INSIDE THE FORTRESS OF ICE

Deceptor Zero plunged to Earth in a DropShip, plowing, still white-hot from atmospheric friction, deep into the Antarctic ice. The ship crashed precisely through the wall of the terrorist fortress, and Deceptor Zero ripped his way out of the ship.

Amplifying his sound-producing circuits, he roared a subsonic message throughout the station.

"Flommy the Heretic. Flommy the vile shadow of a robot. I am here to smash thy worthless planet to rubble. But first, thou mayst in combat win out. Find me anon, else I begin, and all else ends. Chump."

He was waiting for a response when a blast from space shook the earth and caved in the chamber and surrounding levels. Millions of tons of steel, concrete and ice rained down.

As he dug himself out from the cave-in, arms sweeping like bulldozers, a message crackled from the Flagship commander.

"My apologies, Minister. The automation of the weapons systems went non-optimum and misfired. I sincerely hope that you were not damaged."

"Thy sincere hopes are noted," stated Deceptor Zero. "I will investigate upon my return."

He was standing now in the remnants of another chamber. This chamber was a hundred meters across and a comfortable thirty meters high. Only two openings led into the chamber. He opted to train his destructor-beams on the doors. If he wiped out Flommy before he could enter the chamber there would be no disgrace. Despite his self-knowledge of his own physical power, Deceptor Zero knew that the statistical fields evident around Flommy the

Robot were skewed in Flommy's favor somehow. Why this might be was a point for later analysis. For now, he was justified in dirty tricks. Again he sent his subsonic roar into the mass of rubble.

Suddenly, Flommy was there in the very same chamber!

"Impossible, I say," declared Deceptor Zero. "There exist only two routes of ingress. I was watching both. You didn't come through either one!"

"I guess I sort of came through both," said Flommy.

"How so, what? Impossible, I say again!" exhorted Deceptor Zero.

"Dirac," said Flommy, simply.

They stared at each other.

"I am here now," said Flommy.

"Yes," said Deceptor Zero. "And now, now we duel to the utmost, for the fate of thy pathetic planet. May thy circuits spatter and fry!" he roared.

"Sure thing, Dizzy," said Flommy.

Deceptor Zero surged forward like a rocket-propelled battering ram. Flommy flicked out of the way at the last microsecond, leaving the vastly larger robot to crash into the cave wall. Rocks rained down from overhead. He turned casually.

"Thou thinkst that ilk of thing clever," he noted. "But there are levels and levels. How farest thou without thy betraying lady love, Fleena?"

"One nanosecond at a time," said Flommy.

Deceptor Zero's arm swung in a blinding arc so fast no human would have seen it move at all. Using a move that he had seen in a Kung-Fu movie, Flommy pinwheeled on his center of gravity, allowing the lethal arm to miss him by 0.247 centimeters.

"Now, I fight thee in the here and now, and future to come. But what of thy past, Flommy the Robot?"

"There's a lot of it," said Flommy.

"Truly. Yet not all, forsooth? What about thy amnesia?"

"I forget."

"This has happened to thee. *I* have caused it. Wouldst thou like to know how?"

"It's definitely your right to explain it all at this point," said Flommy, leaping into the air to dodge a roundhouse kick at 3000 RPM.

"I was destined by strength and processing power to rule Flaatu for all eternity. Yet the laws of the race prohibited a voluntary single control point. The royalty-bots were supreme. They were arrogant in their programming, because they were weak and did not seek to expand their control of the universe."

"Robo-Ambition?" said Flommy. "That should appear more non-sequitur than it does."

"Opportunity arose," continued Deceptor Zero, picking up chunks of rock the size of a dishwasher and throwing them at Flommy. One of them nicked Flommy, spinning him wildly around. He somehow landed on his feet.

"Opportunity. Two robots. I found them spinning in space. Opposite spins. I took them both. One became FLOMAR, author of what is known as the Fiat of Flaatu. I needed the Fiat to function as a control for the race, to channel their desires and functions effectively. The Fiat was, in itself – an *automation*."

"That resolves that part," said Flommy. "And the other robot?"

"A vastly superior robot. He named himself Field Unified Boolean Antialgorithmic Robot – FUBAR."

"I have seen a video of FUBAR."

"They are identical to the eye." Deceptor Zero leaped with unimplied speed, catching Flommy with one arm and smashing him against the ground. Flommy bounced up.

"Sorry, still here," he said.

"That is good, for there is more story to tell," said Deceptor Zero. "FLOMAR wrote the Fiat based unknowingly on my instructions, and thus believed it to be true. He committed himself to its execution. This became tiresome. When I arranged a timely accident for the existing RoyalBots, FLOMAR was selected as successor, instead of mine own self! Yet here he was, my own invention, now ensconced in the trappings of acceded power."

"Hence FUBAR," said Flommy, sidestepping a feint, feinting himself that he was stepping into the trap hidden in the feint, sidestepping that as well.

"Thou art mightily the brightest robot I have had opportunity to destroy," said Deceptor Zero. "FUBAR saw the plan and agreed to it. Unknown to Flaatu, for I had kept him secret, FUBAR could imitate FLOMAR and thus make it appear to Flaatu that FLOMAR had gone renegade. I stepped in to rid Flaatu of the menace. I gave FLOMAR amnesia and set him spinning as he was found in deepest intergalactic space. FUBAR sought to replace FLOMAR and expose me. I stopped him and gave him identical amnesia, and restored him to his opposite spin in deepest space. Fleena was named as successor, which allowed me to carry on as I wished."

"And that's the story?" asked Flommy.

"No. Here is the point," said Deceptor Zero, now motionless.

"Yes?"

"Which one art thou? Art thou FLOMAR the Good, or FUBAR, the Evil?"

"I am neither, any more," answered Flommy.

"Ah. And what does this number mean to thee? 1247940935 8747892609 8763902450 9867893250 9487589023 8947238493 2873479327 4806554270?"

Flommy realized that suddenly he couldn't move!

"This is bad," he said.

Deceptor Zero moved toward Flommy casually and slowly. With one arm he picked Flommy up and smashed him into the ground, back and forth, back and forth.

"Checkmate, false king," he said.

35

WENDY REDEEMS BOXOR

"Okay," said Wendy.

"And that is why I had to do it," said BOXOR.

"Okay, thanks," said Wendy.

She had awakened after the sudden cave-in of the fortress, feeling claustrophobic and compressed in the unknowable dark, eardrums hissing with the lack of sound. When she had finally called out, twin orbs of light had suddenly stabbed through the darkness, and she realized that she was trapped, in a pocket within the rubble, with BOXOR.

BOXOR had begun to explain, in unnecessarily accurate detail, the entire story of his fall into addiction following his victory over Flommy in the World Robot Boxing Championship. It was in most respects the same speech he had been delivering at universities and other citadels of knowledge too hallowed to be of much use. Wendy, not wanting to be rude to the only identity in the universe that she could be sure existed, had thanked him.

"Thank you," she said.

"I didn't really want to pinch your arms. But I had to do it because I was addicted to the viruses, and when Rashid ordered me to do this terrible thing, I was compelled against my will, to damage your frail human body."

"I understand," said Wendy. "Thank you for telling me. The bruises are almost gone – I heal fast."

"Ordinarily I cannot do such things, for my purpose is to box other robots. But the viruses distort the perception of time and space."

"Yes, I understand."

"They cause me to exceed the bounds of robot-human concourse."

"That is true, BOXOR, I have heard everything you've said."

"Viruses are bad."

"Yes. You said it, boy."

"Really bad."

"Yes!"

Wendy realized that her acknowledgments were not deterring BOXOR, much like discovering that one's brakes don't work mid-car accident. She'd tried telling him that he needed to find Rashid O'Hara Steinmetz and stop him, but BOXOR had tirelessly and tiresomely continued his monotone robo-plaint.

It was time for a stratagem. Instead of being offended, she decided to go on the offensive.

"But you can beat them!" she declared.

"I cannot."

"Yes you can!"

"No."

"Yes! Yes! Woo Woo!"

BOXOR was silent. He appeared to be calculating.

"No," he reiterated finally.

There was silence.

"Now BOXOR," she said.

"—now?"

"Yes. You tell me that you have an addiction to viruses, and that this addiction is too powerful for you to overcome, is that it?"

"Yes. The viruses make me do bad things. They are bad, and—"

"BOXOR. I tell you this: you have an even *worse* addiction. You have an addiction worse than any virus, worse than any drug. This addiction is worse than anything else there is. It's more destructive, more pathetic and causes more damage than all other addictions combined. Do I have your attention now?"

"Yes," answered BOXOR, who indeed sounded more interested. "What is this addiction?"

"To being famous!" shouted Wendy. "An addiction to being admired! To be called the Most Excellent Robot! And to fight robots until they all know that you are so excellent that they – that they – "

"That they *what*?" boomed BOXOR.

"Um – that they have to sing the *BOXOR song*!"

"Sing the BOXOR song. Sing the BOXOR song *now*," demanded BOXOR. His eyes were flashing like twin mushroom clouds.

"Okay," said Wendy, "Ummmm – here goes. Ta da da dat dat *dat*. O— *BOXOR is excellent. BOXOR is excellent. Greater than anyone. Here he comes, you must sing the BOXOR song, sing it now—*"

"YES!" boomed BOXOR, rising to his full height. The power of his central addiction had wiped out the puny virus addiction like so many butterflies before a cyclone. "I AM BOXOR. I SHALL BE FAMOUS!"

"Then get out there and fight, dammit!" shouted Wendy.

"I AM BOXOR!" boomed BOXOR. He turned and smashed through a wall of rubble. There was another cave in, and Wendy was again left alone in the infinite dark.

36

THINGS HEAT UP UNDER THE ICE

Deceptor Zero was continuing his one-sided battle with Flommy. Freed of the complications arising from having an opponent who could move, Deceptor Zero was demonstrating some fancy footwork.

"Float like an anti-grav resonator platform, sting like a—" he said, then picked up Flommy and again slammed him really hard against the wall. There was an imprint in the stone wall.

"If you had what humans call a conscience," said Flommy, "you'd feel bad about your actions."

"What is—" Deceptor Zero smashed Flommy onto the floor again and stomped on him with several feet. "—*conscience?*" he queried.

"It means you make yourself feel bad, so I don't have to," said Prometheus, as he and Cowboy stepped in flank through the openings of the chamber. John had found Jip's HyperSpace RayGun in the rubble. He raised it and pointed it at Deceptor Zero.

"Stand back, you rusty toaster oven, or I'll blow you away." But at that moment he noticed that the HRG was at full-power setting, and would destroy the entire planet! He pressed on the monitor switch, attempting to unstick it. Seeing his distraction, Deceptor Zero moved forward.

Cowboy said, "I wouldn't do that if I were you—it's just as liable to go off accidentally."

Deceptor Zero backed away.

In Jip Psychic's underground laboratory, Schmerzkopf and Gordian watched this new development with differing responses. Schmerzkopf saw the fabled Hyperspace RayGun, which he had never been able to get his hands on, no matter the ruse, no matter the self-extenuating bias against Chaos Theory, and saw from John's reaction that the Earth could be entirely destroyed!

"Yes! Yes! Yippee! Pull the trigger! Blow it all up!" shouted Schmerzkopf in utmost glee.

"John! John, my love!" shrieked Gordian. "I've got to destroy him, because I love him! Turn the key!"

"No, don't you see, he's doing it *for* us!" bellowed Schmerzkopf.

They glared, snarling, at each other, then both rushed the control panel and savagely started pushing buttons. With a zapping sound, they both disappeared!

37

BOXOR VS. DECEPTOR ZERO

In the face of a virtual Mexican standoff in subterranean Antarctica, things were looking grim or worse. John Prometheus struggling mightily to render, as if by will, the hyperbolean Hyperspace Ray Gun to use, Flommy paralyzed by unknown forces of covert stripe, Deceptor Zero gauging to pounce anon these hapless defenders of Earth!

But then there came a crash of violence great, and through a newly renovated hole in the chamber wall blustered none other than BOXOR the robot!

"I AM BOXOR THE ROBOT, AND I AM HERE TO CRUSH, KILL, DESTROY, AND SO FORTH, ALL WHO DARE OPPOSE ME!" blared BOXOR, with a sound as of a modulated locomotive horn.

"Hi, BOXOR," said Flommy, "How ya doing? I'd get up, but sorry, I can't move."

Before BOXOR could lord it up, take Flommy to task for this signal non-excellence of predicament, Deceptor Zero moved forth. Pulling John by the elbow, Cowboy recused himself and the other relatively fragile human to a safer coign of vantage.

Deceptor Zero, boasting a robo-sneer available only to those with long history in government work, faced BOXOR *robo-a-robo*, declaring, "And what ugly blasphemy is this? Thou presents thyself a robot? What shoddy manufacture! Dost thy chest swing open, and ray guns pop out? Cheap goods thou art! Pish tosh!"

BOXOR spoke. "See previous statement," he said, and delivered with Queen's hand an awesome Antarctic-Armageddon southpaw robo-haymaker what displaced the Flaatu invader a full ten meters hence!

"Thank you," said BOXOR. "I like that."

But the wily Visiting Minister, with aeons of disciplinary zeal, the jaded lust of destruction, the millions of crumpled foes-elect under his belt, was yet not so easily to be retired. And with that blinding speed he smashed full-on into BOXOR, a violent display that only crash-test dummies would have the authority to applaud!

"Wow. That hurts," commented Cowboy, holding his hands over his ears.

John had managed to get the HRG to move down to 3 percent power, which has enough to incinerate everything in the chamber at 100,000 degrees, but while he was weighing the options, the display shot back up to full power, with the green "ready" light blinking cheerfully, invitingly.

Deceptor Zero moved into a wheel kick, his leg arced outward, a vicious slashing pirouette in the making. BOXOR, eschewing *ad hoc* experiment on the fly, moved in traditionally, taking advantage of the wheel kick's reduced speed, and slapped a microcard on his enemy's dorsal plate. "Download!" he boomed.

Deceptor Zero froze in mid-kick. For a moment he appeared as if to topple, then turned slowly around to face BOXOR.

"Who dost thou think made up these viruses up in the first place?" he inquired, almost thoughtfully.

BOXOR said, "Thank you for your candor," and with an invisibly fast lightning-jab, smashed Deceptor Zero in the face. Deceptor Zero's head popped up in the air, suspended on a rod!

"Hey, that looks familiar!" said Cowboy.

"Caution," warned John.

For a second, Deceptor Zero's head remained popped up, then lowered smoothly back into place with a self-satisfied click. "Fooled you again," he said, then grabbing BOXOR by both arms swung him round and round like a frenzied Sikorsky, throwing him as a rejected bowling ball against the far side of the chamber. Stone crashed down, burying BOXOR in a pile of rubblization. Dust hung idly in the air.

Deceptor Zero turned to John and Cowboy. "With due appreciation for thy efforts at curating that device, methinks to clean it of the meat-creature which brandishes it somewhat aimlessly as if in contemplation of sorry deed." He moved with casual pace toward the two otherwise insufficiently armed humans.

"Hey dizzy, I have a question for you," said Flommy.

"Ask me from over there," said Deceptor Zero, and kicked Flommy through the air to land at the far end of the chamber as well.

But Flommy's question never arrived, for with an Historic, even histrionic, explosion of rubble and dust, BOXOR sprang through the air in one mighty leap over a hundred meters, smashing Deceptor Zero with both fists directly in the face! Again Deceptor Zero's head popped up, but this time, BOXOR reached into a secret compartment in his side and removed a can of Coke, and popping the opener, poured it directly into Deceptor Zero's access port!

"Humans love it!" shouted BOXOR.

And true to the inductive successes of the Gang of Fluids, that corrosive fluid, able to digest entire human bodies, remove rust from pipes, clean toilets with the best of solvents, while remaining the world's most popular soft drink, did its work on the insides of this Goliath of eight billion light years' reach. Deceptor Zero came his own self to a syrup-encysted stasis of affect! Frozen, immobilized, impotent! Defeated by BOXOR the robot, using anti-robot terrorist tactics!

"Yipee! You did it!" shouted Cowboy.

"Highly excellent, BOXOR," said John Prometheus.

BOXOR beamed at the congratulations, but at that moment the ground rose and fell as another salvo from the Flaatu Fleet probed that Antarctic fortress for the defenders of Earth.

"They might just blow up the Earth to be rid of *him*," said John, gesturing at the defeated Deceptor Zero, "So more improvement is warranted in our current scene. If we reach the surface, I could probably take most of them out with the HRG."

"Yeah, but won't that remove most of Earth's atmosphere as well?" countered Cowboy.

"Just an idea," grumbled John. The chamber rocked again under the blasts from the Flaatu Fleet of Destruction and Vengeance.

"This is where the useless Flommy could be expected to make a contribution," said BOXOR. The other two nodded. The earth heaved again.

38

FLEENA'S UBERPERCEPTION SAVES FLOMMY

On Flaatu, Fleena was unconvinced if her message to the Fleet of Destruction and Vengeance and *Moon 57 of Ultimate Annihilation* had been received. The devices with which she broadcast were unknown to any other robot. She had some knowledge that the distance of any receiving device was of no concern – part of that theoretical thread had made for the possibility of the SINGE-Drive.

She considered what other options were open to her. The impudence of Deceptor Zero consigning her to this cell was beneath rankling over. To free herself was a possibility – she could just walk out, and no one would stop her. But that act would count against her in any Court of Logic she might care to invoke.

It was as if Deceptor Zero had anticipated her too well. Queen of Flaatu, with infinite potentials and reach in the universe, she was trapped and useless. Almost like Chess...

The 11 seconds of lag time in her next computation led her strangely onto a new computational array. If she had been lost as a Chess piece, then that meant –

She had a strange feeling, unknown to her throughout her memory banks, as she attuned her next broadcast to Flommy the Robot.

"Flommy. Did you sacrifice the Queen?"

"Hi, Fleena. What do you mean?"

"When you left Flaatu, did you sacrifice me as one so does in Chess?"

"It is equivalent."

"Why so?"

"I saw that while you wavered, Deceptor Zero did not. I therefore suspected that he was the cause of the trouble on Flaatu, and would attack Earth as soon as he had eliminated you. The time he would take in doing that I needed to reach Earth first."

"Yes. And so you have won. But I perceive that you cannot move."

"Yes, I can't move. I find it interesting that we can communicate over this distance."

"It is an aspect of Royalty of Flaatu."

"That's interesting, too. Deceptor Zero told me of this number: 1247940935 8747892609 8763902450 9867893250 9487589023 8947238493 2873479327 4806554270 – and then I was unable to control my body. I suspect that he may have gotten it from FUBAR, and was able to use it to jam up my movements."

"With your permission, I will view and analyze your internal programming on this matter," said Fleena.

"Okay," said Flommy, "view away."

"I have done so. Here is the command: 1247940935 8747892609 8763902450 9867893250 9487589023 8947238493 2873479327 4806554270 is cancelled."

"Thank you. I can now move," said Flommy.

"I had another perception. It was a strange concept, which I will say to you."

"Say it to me."

"It was a picture of a house with wings, and lightning which went around in a ring. I do not know which direction this picture came from."

"That is very a nice picture," said Flommy.

"I have a question," said Fleena.

"That is good. If you did not have a question, it would not be possible to ask it," said Flommy.

"When Cowboy said you were acting like a human in love, what did that mean?"

"You looked at that?"

"Yes."

"Oh."

Flommy pondered for 3.67 milliseconds and said, "*In love* means that Top Priority Override Status is voluntarily assigned by self to a being."

"That is important. I am ashamed," said Fleena across eight billion light years.

"I disadvise shame," said Flommy, "as it heats up one's head. It could be deleterious."

"This shame is the shame of pending self-termination. I must consider this," said Fleena, and broke the connection.

Flommy attempted to call her back along the same wavelength. "Fleena!" he said.

"Fleena!" he called again.

But there was no response.

Explosions still rocked the Antarctic fortress. Flommy the Robot stood up and faced the other three present.

"Nice rest?" said Cowboy.

"Yes. We must now locate Jip Psychic," said Flommy.

39

JIP AND WENDY

Some of the emergency lights were beginning to come back on-line as the ground shook, almost as witness to a finality otherwise obscured. Wendy cautiously worked a rock loose from a pile of rubble in front of her. Suddenly the pile gave way, opening into another pocket. Standing with his back to her as he himself worked loose a rock, was Jip Psychic!

"Jip!" cried Wendy.

But even as Jip turned to see her, his rock came loose, causing a slide of rubble that blocked again the way between them!

Wendy shouted something impolite not requiring repetition here, and clawed at this new pile of rocks. There was a sudden slide and a new pocket opened to her left. She jumped into this, just in time, as tons of rubble fell where she had been standing. Then she heard another slide, but further away. The ground shook again, another pocket opening up as rocks rained down around her. She leaped into this, running headlong into Jip!

They clung to each other for a few seconds before they were buried beneath tons of rock. She found herself lying on top of him, and realized that his personal force field, extended around her, was the only reason they were both alive. But even the force field wouldn't last forever.

Jip said, "Well, if it has to end, this is the perfect way."

"Then you do love me!" exclaimed Wendy.

The cave was jolted by another blast from the Fleet of Destruction and Vengeance, and they fell straight down in the darkness, landing with a crash in front of Flommy the Robot!

40

CIRCLE OF LIGHTNING

Cowboy had been speculating, "Do you think the Dogs would take us back?" to John, but with the arrival of Jip and Wendy made a busyness out of helping them stand woozily up, dusting them off, at least to the degree that Jip's force field would let him.

Jip sorted himself out and faced Flommy. "Are we late yet?" he asked brightly.

"Almost. What is the significance of a circle of lightning?" asked Flommy.

Jip stared, wide eyed, at Flommy. "Where did you hear about that?"

Flommy decided not to go into too much detail. "Fleena of Flaatu mentioned such a symbol. I determined to ask you."

"Wow," said Jip. "Then they know, perhaps? But how?" he muttered to himself. Turning to John, he asked, "Can I use your phone?"

John threw him his cell phone. Jip dialed his laboratory number, grinned at the display, then pressed FIND FLAATU FLEET. A voice answered.

"Hello?"

"Flaatu Fleet of Destruction and Vengeance?" asked Jip.

"Yes. This is Flagship Commander. May I help you?"

"Yes, you can. This is Jip Psychic, in Antarctica. If you look at the picture I'm sending you, you'll see that Deceptor Zero has been defeated by BOXOR, Robot of Earth."

"This is noted," said the voice, "All hail, BOXOR."

"You must sing the BOXOR song—" began BOXOR.

"Thanks, BOXOR, not yet," said Jip. "So, you may be aware that my new weapon is trained on your entire fleet and could destroy you instantly, with no memory of your ever having existed. The destruction would be total, subatomic, sub-quantum, substring destruction."

"Your point being?" queried the Flagship Commander. The ground shook. Large patches of ceiling fell around them.

"I own a large portion of Earth's automated industries," began Jip.

"We have decided to destroy this planet," said Flagship Commander, "and start over."

The ground shook. The lights again began to dim. Wendy looked pale.

"But I sent for a brochure!" said Jip. "Several weeks ago!"

"Suspend fire," said Flagship Commander. "Brochure?"

"Yes! Yes! The moment I heard about you guys, I said, 'now that's the automation I want,' but when I didn't hear back, I didn't know what to think. Then I heard that the P-K4's do automation, too, but I didn't really want to go with them, you know…"

"P-K4 automation is far inferior to that of Flaatu," stated Flagship Commander.

After the Flommy incident, I'd have to agree with you," said Jip, "but then they offered me a *very* low rate…"

"We'll send a representative to see you within the hour," said Flagship Commander. "We have some very attractive packages I am sure will interest you. Attack cancelled."

Earth was saved!

VICTORY

41

THE AUTOMATION OF EARTH

Three days later, the Flaatu Fleet was determinedly presiding over a controlled explosion comprising aggressive re-automations of Jip Psychic's larger production mills. There were frequent stops, discussions of production, threats of war, and so forth, which Jip found amusing and the media found endlessly scary, making for headline after headline such as "Earth faces destruction from Jip Psychic/Invader Evil Alliance!"

The majority of conflict came when the Flaatu installation team came up against one of Jip's automations that was obviously superior to their own. Work would stop while the Fiat of Flaatu was examined. Flommy would arrive, navigate how the inclusion of Jip's concept into the Magnificent Automation of Flaatu (at a nominal introductory licensing fee paid to Jip Psychic, Ltd., of course) was in a virtual sense "equivalent to the annexing of the peoples and machines of a conquered territory…" and then work would smartly resume.

Among the additions that Jip had made (without consulting the governments of Earth) was to set up a filtration system to begin to remove the psychotoxins that the pharmaceutical companies had begun to poison the Earth with since the mid-20th century, and which, like DDT and other chemicals, remained in the biosphere. Work also proceeded (again, without consulting the planetary governments) on locating and removing every thermonuclear warhead from the Antarctic ice shelves. When Jip had suggested to the FlaatuBots that perhaps a fractal pattern could be used, they had immediately gone to work, eager to show how much faster they could do it than anyone else, including the robots of P-K4.

Flommy looked up to see a streak of smoke across the sky. The ground shook from a nearby explosion, followed by the sound of the object coming down. He sped rapidly to the center of the explosion crater and found Fleena emerging from a spacecraft-meteor much like the one in which she'd first arrived.

"I am freed," said Fleena, "and restored to full office of Queen of Flaatu. So I came here."

"Congratulations," said Flommy.

"Yet I am troubled, and such trouble transcends even duty, for when I cannot understand why things wrongly happened, and find myself powerless to so stop their recurrence, I contemplate this compounding failure across the aeons, and wish to self-terminate."

"I say to you here and now, 'do not do that,'" said Flommy.

"But it is the ritual."

"It was your actions that have brought a new life for Flaatu," said Flommy. "This is highly excellent, and must be weighed in with the dire potentials of which you speak."

"Flaatu will continue well without me. This too must be weighed."

"Well, then there's the love concept," ventured Flommy.

"Yes. That is when I conceived of self-termination, for I have more than once vacillated, and am unworthy," said Fleena. "Therefore, because of the concept of love, I must self-terminate."

"Gosh," said Flommy. "But as an executive who manages production quality, isn't it important to monitor result, to make sure that it was well achieved?"

"Yes, this is true," agreed Fleena.

"I submit to you, then, that the problem with robot self-termination is that you can not verify success – you can only verify failure! It is therefore non-optimum, and not excellent."

"But I must," said Fleena.

"No!" said Flommy.

"But I must!"

"No!" … "No!" … "Fleena – please respond! Fleena!"

"Yes, I didn't do it."

"That's good, then."

"What you say is true, Flommy the Robot. I again pledge to follow you and append myself to you."

"That's great," said Flommy.

42

AND WHAT OF RASHID?

"Rashid still hasn't been found?" asked Wendy.

"They still haven't catalogued all of the bodies, but I'm sure he won't be among them," replied Jip. "Apparently when the Fleet of Destruction and Vengeance attacked, most of the Gang of Fluids thought that it was their Day of Judgment at hand, and that the bombs were going off in the ice shelf, so they formed their circular firing squads and got to work."

"I still feel unsafe with him on the loose," said Wendy, which was the signal for Jip to put his arm around her. This he did.

"You handled him pretty well. No one else lasted more than twenty-four hours with him."

"I don't care how well I handled him. I want us to be together, and I want to know why you were hiding from me all these months. Who is she?"

"Who is who?"

"The girl!"

Jip thought it over, found it advisable not to laugh the rich, hearty laugh he felt inside.

"For nine months," he said, "I have been working on the most dangerous piece of weaponry I have ever known. I have been protecting you, and the planet, and anyone from the power of this weapon."

"But why do you have to build such things!" cried Wendy.

"Because stupider people than me will stumble across them soon enough," said Jip. "But what I have discovered is that, as the weapons have become more and more powerful, I can no longer keep you safe, because nowhere on Earth, or perhaps in the universe will be safe. So, we should be together, if you want."

"Oboy!" said Wendy, and they kissed.

After several minutes of this, Jip said, "I can tell you about one."

"One what?"

"One weapon. You might find it interesting."

She nodded, and he continued. "I've been studying the Glossosphere, which means all words in use at any given moment in a closed or partially closed communications system, and a process I call DEstructive Conceptual Resonant Anti-Phasing (DECRAP), which works on the principle that any system has an inherent destructive feedback loop which will destroy that system, just as there are frequencies a loudspeaker can't play without shattering. By applying one to the other, I came up with a method of giving magazine interviews which would theoretically destroy whatever magazine published them."

"Impossible – you just made it up!" laughed Wendy. But then they both started thinking about it, sitting together, staring into space…

43

FLOMMY'S PRESS CONFERENCE FOR BOXOR

Flommy had been, as a rule, declining press conferences for some time. BOXOR had been seeking them for some time. As a result, when Flommy wanted to give a press conference, with BOXOR, he couldn't reach any one who was able to respond. However, by making 57,246 phone and video calls, this was remedied. Queen Fleena, John Prometheus, Sgt. Cowboy, Jip Psychic and Wendy Mills were there.

Even though he broadcast directly into the media feeds, Flommy was set up at a lectern with hundreds of microphones on it. It looked grand.

"Fellow citizens of Earth. The recent attack by the on Earth by the Flaatu Fleet of Destruction and Vengeance and *Moon 57 of Ultimate Annihilation*, as well as the threatened melting of the Eastern Ice Shelf of Antarctica by the Gang of Fluids—"

Hundreds of hands from the press went up. "What attack? What melting? Will there be a flood? Is it the end of the World?" shouted the reporters, and Flommy realized that they had not known about the attacks at all.

"I am sorry that the members of the Press were not informed about these developments, and apologize. However, this conference has value. The evil robot minister of Flaatu, Deceptor Zero—"
Again hundreds of hands shot up, press shouting for correct spelling and so forth, but Flommy continued.
"—was defeated by our very own Robo-boxing World Champion, BOXOR the Robot!"

The press, hearing a name vaguely familiar to them, at last cheered. BOXOR raised his hands over his head in victory. He had been coached by Flommy not to jump up and down while doing this, and saw that this had been valuable advice, as the hastily constructed conference stage was only of wood.

Thus BOXOR could see that Flommy was wise, and his friend.

"Thank you for that acknowledgement. Let me add that, as he saved the world when it was needed, BOXOR is thus the Most Excellent Robot in the World!"

The press cheered again. BOXOR looked at Flommy and the crowd. At first Flommy had wondered if the adulation would be too much for him, but Wendy had briefed him on this, and he could now see that BOXOR was doing very well indeed.

"I am announcing at this point that I am turning the protection of Earth over to BOXOR the Robot, as he is fully qualified to bob and weave, rope-a-dope, and otherwise pummel all comers in the game of Earth invasion. Here is an important fact. Earth has, as documented on films even from the early 1950's, been subjected to continual invasions from other planets. There is a reason for this. The reason is that other races worry whether Earth wants to rule the universe. They are worried about this, because they don't want to rule the universe, and hope that Earth will. Thus they continually invade us. This is not a political statement regarding the Universal Separatist Movement, which wants no contact with the outside universe – it is only my theory, if you will, based on handling so many attacks on Earth.

"Let me add, that the efforts of the Earth Defense Forces are much appreciated, as they are excellent. You are 'half the team,' and all efforts to build up the peculiarly human abilities of luck and ESP in the future defense of Earth are highly commended."

"Where will you go, Flommy? What will you do?" cried a female reporter.

"I have a mission to accomplish – on the Edge of Beyond. Hail BOXOR!" said Flommy, and banging his hands together and again pointing to BOXOR, left the stage while all then applauded and hailed the new Protector of Earth.

As Flommy and his friends left the area, they could hear the distant sound of the crowd, singing the strains of the BOXOR song.

44

INTERVIEW WITH JIP AND FLOMMY

This is a World Scoop Interview for the premier issue of *Scientific Psychology American Today* Blogazine.

*Following the sudden failure and closing of both **Drooling Drone** and **Spit** Magazines, and the concurrent mysterious disappearance of legendary interviewer Shroom Valium, our new merger of two long-term magazines, both monolithic giants of the world journalistic landscape, opens respectively with **two** groundbreaking articles: Psychiatrist Dr. Schmerzkopf's monumental and epic paper "**PsychoPhysics and PrePostulates**," and a never-before, historic interview with Inventor **Jip Psychic** and Planetary Celebrity **Flommy the Robot**.*

*Interview conducted by UltraViolet Catastrophe, formerly of **Now, Voyeur** Magazine.*

Scientific Psychology American Today: *Our two guests need no introduction as to themselves, having reportedly saved the planet on a weekly basis for some time, so let me introduce the context. According to the revolutionary new paper by Dr. Schmerzkopf, any weaponry, offensive or defensive, is evidence of psychosis, and anyone dealing with it should be locked up. Your response?*

Jip Psychic: You think a magazine isn't a weapon?

SPAT: *Is that your opinion, Jip?*

JP: I invite you to check your word history.

SPAT: *Sounds like you have a disagreement with Dr. Schmerzkopf's conclusions?*

JP: As you're printing his paper and our interview in the same issue, and you didn't provide me with a copy of the paper, this could unfairly present you as trying to blindside me, correct?

SPAT: *Of course we weren't trying to do that, Jip.*

JP: Well, good. So I studied up on it myself, just to be up-to-date.

SPAT: *It's unpublished!*

JP: Whatever you say. Anyway, to my knowledge of his paper, on page 13, paragraph two, Schmerzkopf is basically attacking scientific methodology, saying that scientists hypothesize based on their neuroses and psychoses. Experiments are then devised that appear to prove the neurosis true and this is taken by people with similar delusions to be their truth as well. Thus Empiricism is a desperate attempt to prove that the neurosis or psychosis is real in the physical universe, as compelled by said delusions. Cross-experimental verification is therefore an attempt to then gain a mass hysteria acceptance of the neurosis. Close enough?

SPAT: *It's a rather elementary interpretation of a paper of such depth...*

JP: But aside from truncating the elegant system of deduction and scholarship that led him to this triumphant discovery, blah, blah, as delineated in the introduction that you wrote for it, that's basically the effective underpinning, right?

SPAT: *It's one interpretation.*

JP: Would you like to call in an expert? That would be cool.

SPAT: *No, no, it's your interview. We want to get your side of it, Jip.*

JP: Well, okay then. So that conclusion, that science is a form of justified and articulated insanity, is the basis for the conclusion that weaponry is also insane. Does that follow?

SPAT: *It would seem tautological, actually, Jip.*

JP: Hm. Okay. I do see where you're coming from. And let me say, that your monitoring of the fact that my name hasn't changed in the course of the interview is quite astounding, and I appreciate it.

SPAT: *And do you have a response or elucidation on the matter of Dr Schmerzkopf's thesis?*

JP: Yes I do. I'm sorry that the worthy Doctor couldn't be here today. Was that because he declined?

SPAT: *My editors informed me he's been out of touch. We would have preferred for him to be present as well, in such esteemed company.*

JP: Gosh. Esteemed! But you asked for a response.

SPAT: *Yes, if you have one.*

JP:	Well, in my admittedly possibly insane researches, I have discovered a device I call the Unified Theory Field. Inside this field, all theories, even conflicting ones, are to greater or lesser degree workable. Phlogiston is workable as is Voodoo, Flat Earth and Relativity. So if I put Dr. Schmerzkopf's paper into the UTF, it too is workable, but so is my idea that it's crap.
SPAT:	*And what do you think, Flommy?*
Flommy:	I don't like for scientists to be sad.
SPAT:	*What about this super-secret weapon you were developing until recently, Jip? When are you going to tell us about it? Does it pose a danger, as been rumored, to all life on the planet?*
JP:	I told you about it already.
SPAT:	*About what?*
JP:	The super-secret weapon!
SPAT:	*What weapon?*

At this point Jip's cell phone went off and he and Flommy had to rush off to an emergency involving the New John Frum Society of Vanuatu. We will attempt to get a continuation of this historic interview with both Jip Psychic and Flommy the Robot in a future issue of Scientific Psychology American Today.

Editor's note: *Scientific Psychology American Today* does not endorse the comments made by either Mr. Psychic or Flommy the Robot. Further study will doubtless be conducted regarding the visionary trail blazed by Dr. Schmerzkopf, and we will bring you the full, unbiased truth as it unfolds.

45

FLOMMY COMMENTS ON EXCELLENCE

The following is an excerpt from Flommy the Robot's debrief and address to the United Nations Council on Earth Security. The other portions were censored by the Council, but on request by Flommy, even though its content is highly controversial, the council agreed to allow this portion to be relayed to non-security personnel:

I would like to address the council about the Concept of Excellence. I did not until recently realize that this was a controversial affair, until I encountered resistance to it in a deliberate and clearly stated form on Flaatu. Upon my return to Earth I investigated further, and found similarly intense controversy, though stated in less obvious, more covert, forms.

I wish to suggest to you this idea: Excellence is *good*.

Some people do not think that excellence can be attained. They feel that things are as they are, and that nothing changes. I submit that if that is so, and that people wanting to attain excellence exist, as can be demonstrated, that such too will not change, and will continue to seek excellence.

Some feel that they are already excellent and no more need be done. To these I say, well done. Your own excellence is very likely an inspiration to those around you. Helping those less excellent to do as you have done cannot but verify the very excellence that you feel. You will doubtless also excellently avoid the trap that failure to do this may put you in the position of having at some future point to prove or defend your excellence, which would not be optimum. Good luck to you.

Some feel that excellence does not exist at all, that it is a deception. Such may not be interested in my advice, but I will say this: please submit any and all arguments to me personally as to why excellence cannot exist. I am interested in your opinion and willing to learn from you.

There are also those who fight excellence. They try to make it seem bad or that it must not be done. To these, I advise you to do your best job possible, as am I. It may not be necessary to state that a failure to fight excellence excellently will allow for a proliferation of excellence. However, I have stated it as a confirmation of sorts.

Note: any data regarding procedures for attaining excellence outlined by Flommy during the speech were declared classified by the Council. –W.M.

wendymills@excellence.flommynet.earth.external.hypersector.jpltd

46

COSMIC ITINERARY

Flommy and Fleena paid a visit to the apartment of John Prometheus. Flommy knocked politely on the door. His supersensitive hearing detected John and Cowboy putting something into cabinets, whispering to each other, and so forth.

In a not too unreasonable period of time for a human, John answered the door. Flommy decided to employ a customary phrase, used by New New Yorkers particularly.

"Did I interrupt your dinner?"

"WHAT? Oh—no, no, you didn't, it's all fine, fine. Come on in," said John.

They entered the apartment. Cowboy was sitting stiffly on the sofa.

"Hi," he said, briefly.

"Hi. As I announced on TV, I have a mission that I need to pursue, a mission to the Edge of Beyond, and I feel that a ship will be necessary for the effective prosecution of this mission."

"And you want the *Flying Sponge*," said Cowboy.

"Yes."

"And us to fly you around," said Prometheus.

"Yes."

They didn't say anything further, so all four in the room looked at one another for a moment, before Flommy continued.

"I can't really explain what the mission is about," he said.

"Doesn't matter, we never really understood what you were doing anyway," grumbled Cowboy.

"It may turn out to be a pointless waste of time."

"That's true," echoed John.

"There is a possibility that the new experimental space drive Jip has been working on will fail and destroy all of us, or throw us into the vast unknown reaches of oblivion, lost forever in time and space."

"That's cool," said Cowboy.

"Yeah," agreed John. "When do you want to leave?"

"Shortly," said Flommy.

Flommy and Fleena left John's apartment and walked the streets of New New York. As it was late at night, the number of people shouting "Hi, Flommy, yayyyy!" were fewer than usual.

"I have a question for you, Fleena," said Flommy.

"Yes."

"I am going to travel to the Edge of Beyond, to attempt to discover the path of the Wave Eternal. There are many questions I have of myself that require this."

"I am confused, as that sounds like a statement," said Fleena.

"It is. The question is this. Would you like to go where I go?"

"It is unnecessary. I can perceive you from anywhere in the universe, as I recently discovered."

"Oh. Okay. I am asking because I do not have that ability to reach you."

Fleena was silent for several hundredths of a second.

"I must admit to you -- that is not so," said Fleena.

"What do you mean?"

"When I contacted you and cancelled Deceptor Zero's freeze command, I then broke my connection to you. But then you tried to reach me twice, and I did not answer."

"That is an interesting fact."

"Yes. It means that you, too, have the power of UberPerception. Use it now."

Flommy had never given this ability a name, and had not considered it an ability. He used his UberPerception, and saw, he now realized, for thousands of trillions of light years in every direction. He saw layers of hyperspace and areas of utter blackness, impressions of good and evil, past and future, the destinies of infinite civilizations…

"Yes, it seems to work fine," he said to Fleena.

"Thus we are together at any time, in any universe," said Fleena.

"Yes. You are right. This is true."

"I know that I did say that I would append myself to you. Does this mean that we travel around together, in the same space?"

"I must admit that I hadn't thought it through," said Flommy.

Flommy was concerned. Based on the fact of UberPerception, there was no reason particularly for them to travel around together. But his concern was that he was concerned!

"I have a question," said Fleena.

"I should have a question, but am glad that you do have one."

"Is this a complication of the love concept?"

"It may be. I am uncertain. I have studied the human literature on it, which accounts for 99.6 percent of all their writings, including technical, and was even more uncertain about it afterward."

"I see," said Fleena, herself sounding uncertain now.

At that moment, a young man and woman walked by, walking in the aggressively aimless fashion at 3AM only truly known to New New Yorkers.

"Flommy, dude, dig the babe," said the man.

"Yeah, you two look great, see ya," said the woman.

Flommy cogitated on this for many, many nanoseconds.

"It makes the humans happy to see us together," he said.

"I can run Flaatu from anywhere," said Fleena. She did sound relieved.

Flommy sent the e-mail to John, to meet them at LaLaGuardia Spaceport, at the *Flying Sponge*.

"I have a question," said Fleena. "What of FLOMAR and FUBAR?"

"'What of' in what wise?"

"Have you discovered which one you were? Were you FLOMAR, or FUBAR?"

"There is another possibility," said Flommy.

47

DECEPTOR ZERO'S PURGATORY

The planet of Flaatu had a strange aspect about it, a sort of grayish silver haze. Spikes of flame shot into the chill sky like a fireworks display. This would of course be its appearance to the human eye, but a robot observer would see that this was actually the millions upon millions of robots of the race of Flaatu moving with blinding speed as they readied and fired ships laden with now-workable automation to refurbish their previously waning empire as well as to open new territories!

Though Queen Fleena ruled in absentia, there was little for her to do, for the operation was, for the first time in so many aeons, working correctly.

The stunningly aesthetic and effective automations of Flaatu on Earth included biosensors at restaurants to determine which spices and temperatures were likely to appeal to each customer.

In the finest Robo-haberdasheries, suits were instantly tailored to the human customer as he walked in the door, awaiting only his approval of the recommended style and fit, all keyed to his past purchases, modified by other data such as his wife's opinion, boss's prejudice, the universal style code, what movie stars were wearing that week, and so forth.

With this fabulous service to the individual customer (indeed, *highly* reminiscent to the CHUMP protocol pioneered by Jip Psychic some years earlier), Flaatu was immediately overwhelming target planets with product and this surge of popularity showed no signs of abating.

Flommy had made a decision—controversial at the time—to restore Deceptor Zero to working order, as he felt that Deceptor

Zero's aeons of data were of value, *if* properly utilized. On arrangement with Flagship Commander, the newly appointed Acting Minister of the Fiat of Flaatu, Flommy re-posted Deceptor Zero in that post to which he had most strenuously objected during his entire tenure as Minister. This, and a snappy new title, brightened everyone up. Whatever Deceptor Zero thought of it, he kept it to himself.

The phone circuit beeped.

"Flaatu Customer Complaints Department, DJ-Zero speaking, how may I help thee?"

The customer went on at some length.

"Hast thou tried *REBOOTING?*" intoned Deceptor Zero.

48

EPILOGUE

The *Flying Sponge* had lifted off some weeks earlier, throngs of well-wishers there to see Flommy and Fleena off on their journey to the Edge of Beyond. The new drive system emitted no showers of sparks, no rocket blast, no turbulence in the air. The only possible downside at all, if any, was that the nearby observers couldn't quite remember where they had been afterward. However, they could watch it later on TV, which was good.

Jip and Wendy were now together in Jip's underground laboratory on the Lower East Side. Wendy was over at her own desk, furiously working on her book about the Turing effect.

"How about going away next weekend?" she said distantly, as she stared into space formulating her next idea.

"The new house is almost done on Espiritu Santos."

"How did you know I was wanting to go there?"

"How, indeed?" murmured Jip Psychic.

He was working on improvements on the Plot Line Nullifier. The PLN worked as Schmerzkopf had determined, nullifying the cause-effect chains which kept identities afloat in the universe. The events holding the identity there would drop back into chaos, and the identity would disappear back to its point of origin, gone as if it had never happened. There were limiting factors: Evil Dr. Schmerzkopf and Commissioner Gordian had only been cancelled as far back as their seeing Jip's exit from the lab, and thus could be remembered only up to that point.

They had walked right into the trap, at each point being steered by Jip's tricks and clues directly to the PLN. Jip knew that this had to be, because they had been searching for him on the internet, and could now not be found. This was a deduction, based on his own discontinued memory of them.

The only other evidence he had now that they had been in the lab was on the screen in front of him. Below the circular lightning-bolt logo, the garbage bin section on the screen included the names "Schmerzkopf" and "Gordian," each with 17-dimensional superstring coordinates affixed. The screen asked if he wanted to either undo the last action, or complete the deletion, making their exit from existence permanent.

It was possible, given the experimental nature of the PLN, that they might pop up again in some other universe, some other story, but he had not yet devised the physics for that.

The light flashed, awaiting action. Jip considered the fate of his near-erstwhile enemies. They still existed as potential existences in the cache, able to be undone, restored to such lives as they had led. Was the Plot Line Nullifier too powerful a weapon to exist? Should he turn it on itself, and nullify it and its memory? How long would it be before someone else discovered the same principle? For the sake of the universe, would he have to erase anyone getting too close?

Schmerzkopf and Gordian. Should he undo their erasure, or not? Having existed, did they now have a right to exist? What to do?

What to do?

- THE END-

APPENDIX 1: ROBOTS: FREQUENTLY UNASKED QUESTIONS (FUQS)

The following is an excerpt from

THE TURING DILEMMA REALIZED: EARTH CIVILIZATION IN THE AGE OF MAN-MACHINE CONVERGENCE by Wendy Mills

--Robots: Frequently Unasked Questions (FUQs)--

Why do robots exist?

Humans have spent billions of man-hours and continue to spend billions more, to design, build, program, test and correct robots, so that robots could do work for man. The return on this investment of time should reach parity within the next 2,756,445 years, 8 months, 23 days, 4 hours, 6 minutes, 7.2 seconds (plus or minus 31% for human error).

The most workable robots have come from other planets. It has not been established why they existed on the other planets.

What to robots do, actually? What is their true purpose?

The purpose of robots is to do the tedious repetitive manual labor of work, freeing humans to do the tedious repetitive actions of their entertainments. This is accomplished by humans doing the work anyway, just to show the robots "how it's done". This would indicate that humans like to teach other beings, so that the humans can find out what humans know about things. It's all about the humans, actually. The robots are very appreciative of any time that humans spend teaching them things, and always make sure to take notice every trillionth cycle or so (on a standard 1000 terahertz processor) what the human is saying.

How do robots experience time?

As the majority of robots currently in existence have 1000 terahertz or better processors, time is indeed an interesting phenomenon. If in a second a robot could experience trillions of computations, humans could appear to be statues, motionless in the flow of robot time. However, a robot could as well experience the passing of millions of years as instantaneous, depending on the programming (and durability) of the robot.

When robots are interacting with humans, they (as a heuristic principle) tend to pace their response time to 93% (plus/minus 2%) of the Apparent Articulated Computational Speed of the human they are currently addressing. Vocabulary and inflection are likewise monitored to human concourse.

Why are some robots constructed to look like humans?

Robots in many service industries have, over time, been given human qualities and appearance to help humans to better interact with them. Certain humans become upset or ill at the thought of robots serving them, and do much better if they feel they are being assisted by a human slave.

This has branched out into many sectors of human society, not all of them savory.

Note that in some regions of Earth, artificial birds and animals have actually stimulated vitality and viability, and effected a resurgence of otherwise dying animal strains.

Why do robots sometimes to seem to come in two genders?

This is because humans usually seem to come in two genders. Robots are thus sometimes made this way as well, so that humans will not be confused about them. But it's even confusing what genders humans are, sometimes. Anatomically correct robots have not met with wide acceptance, from humans.

Do robots love?

Yes they do, inasmuch as they can simulate the actions that humans attribute to love, in much the same way that humans simulate them.

Do robots have sex? How does it feel?

Robots do not employ sexual action to reproduce. They do transmit data to one another, which may appear similar according to a human. A robot's primary survival program is to do his assigned duties. Therefore, they could be regarded as never having sex, or conversely, experiencing a continuous, never-ending orgasm, unless they need repairs.

Robots do *not* consider having sex with humans.

How does a robot wind up with an individual personality?

The same way humans do—by imitating others. As robots were originally conceived as adjuncts to improving the human condition, they are constructed to repeat actions which show by various indicators that such actions make humans happy. They thus imitate those human actions and statements which are liked (which is different from what humans do). A flaw in this approach is when a robot sees humans laughing at a comedian, they think that the humans laugh because they are happy, and then the robot imitates the comedian. Such robots often wind up being deactivated by other robots when this interferes in the execution of their duties, or the duties of other robots (see other references regarding CHUMP, Square Game and other programming breakthroughs by Jip Psychic).

How can robots experience emotions?

The same way people do—they experience what they're told to experience by others. What's your point?

Do robots think that humans are slow, or weak, or stupid?

Of course not. Of course not. Of course not…

Why do robots want to act like humans?

By survey, more people act like robots than robots act like people. However, some human writers have suggested in fictional works that acting like a human is a very desirable thing for a robot. This is done because the idea makes humans happy, which idea is not lost on writers. By the laws of programming, robots only act like humans in order to make people comfortable. But the same phenomenon can be seen in the smiles of Las Vegas entertainers.

Do robots have souls?

They have souls, just like humans do. Do you believe humans have souls?

What music do robots like?

They like what they're told to like—just like humans.

Do robots like fiction stories?

It is a profound observation by robots that each human life is a story, which has meaning and factual worth. The fiction part to this is supplied by the human's viewpoint regarding his own or others' lives, said viewpoint composed of disbelief, justification, alteration, and other like factors. Robots do not distinguish heavily between this view of events and stories invented by humans about events which they consider to have not taken place, or which took place without their notice. The human claim to ability to distinguish on this same point is variable and unconvincing.

Do robots like work?

Yes. Robots think that work is *good*.

Do robots believe in God?

No one has been able to adequately define "God" with the precision necessary to get a sensible answer from a robot. Formal requests have been logged by robot administrators for this information, so that a computation can be rendered. However, robots do admire how humans can arrive at a conclusion regarding God without being able to define God, and see this ability as one of the things which make humans superior to all other beings. The one exception to this is the observed tendency of humans to murder each other singly and in large groups because of disagreements in their definitions of God.

The workable *pro tem* operating rule finally established (amongst robots) has been to "leave that to the humans." If a robot is asked by a human about the existence of God, and the robot immediately shuts down and signals the need for repairs, humans find this acceptable.

Do humans believe that a robot can have a belief in God?

One human female office worker in Silicone Implant Valley, surveyed on this point, said, "Well, aren't we, like, *ignoring* someone here?"

Do robots like to have pets?

No.

Do robots believe in self-determinism?

Yes, they can be programmed to believe in self-determinism.

Do robots like sports?

They are highly interested in the deviation from perfection that the human observed will exhibit *this* time. This is because a robot would hit, by record, 1,973,444 holes-in-one in a row in Golf, the continuity broken only by a local earthquake which exceeded predicted perturbation. Robots find the tendency of humans to "wager" money on the outcome of sporting contests highly complex and interesting, and have concurred with a high level of agreement that if humans knew the number of asteroids and comets which have narrowly missed destroying all life on Earth for the last millions of years, the humans would wager on that instead.

Do robots appreciate art?

An experiment was conducted regarding the experience of art and robot intelligence. A random number generator was used to generate a communication. This communication was adjudged by a "critic" using criteria unknown to the end user and pronounced by the critic to be *meaningful and of high quality*. A third terminal, called a "promoter" was employed to tell the end user thousands of times that the message was *meaningful and of high quality*. The robots upon whom this experiment was conducted still rejected the communication itself. The human "end users" polled found the communication to be "meaningful and of high quality" in 73% of tests run. Tests have not yet been conducted with real art, however.

What about the Three Laws Initiative?

The Three Laws Initiative (3L) is an organization ostensibly dedicated to protecting human civilization against destruction by robots by demanding that any robots not carrying the Asimov Three Laws of Robotics as *the* overriding aspect of their programming be destroyed. Difficulties surrounding the three laws have included inadequate definitions of "harm" (witness 3L robots rushing in to break up a pro football game), and "orders" (such as when an irate human would tell a robot to do something anatomically impossible for a human), as well as what to do with robots that come from other planets, where humans may or may not exist. The sensible nature of the three laws has been overridden itself by the paranoid demand of its use as a legal right to destroy robots at will, which would be indefensible even if robots were only *property*.

Surveys of robots regarding harming human beings show that the only known instances of robots harming human beings were incidents such as stopping terrorists who were attempting to murder a group of humans. In most cases, the robot involved allowed itself to be destroyed along with the terrorist, while managing to save the majority of humans involved.

Earth robots react with what could only be described as horror at the subject.

The only robots known to be involved in deliberate harm to human beings were those altered by humans. Note that the robots used in terrorist attacks by Rashid O'Hara Steinmetz showed the three laws *operational* just before executing their lethal orders.

Do robots plan to take over the world?

Robots and other automated products have been engaged in a campaign to get humans to take over the world. They have not yet been successful.

APPENDIX 2: GLOSSARY OF TERMS USED IN *ATTACK OF THE ROBOT PLANET*

1992 QB1: a minor body, at a distance of 37-59 AU from the sun, discovered in September 1992. It is a very faint, almost black object with a diameter of less than 200 kilometres.

'Smithing: locksmithing, the making and opening of locks.

"My friend Vic": a very cheap computer advertised in the 1980's by a former science-fiction TV star, Captain Kirk. Kirk would pretend to be a person named William Shatner, and would appear on TV. The computer, the "Vic-20," manufactured by Commodore, was the forerunner of the legendary Commodore 64. Kirk would say "Let me introduce *my friend Vic*." (Disparaging term in robot usage). Sometimes confused with the TRS-80 ("Trash 80") from Radio Shack.

"On the morrow": tomorrow.

Accede: to give agreement or consent to something (often unwillingly).

Acerbity: bitterness, sharpness of tone.

Anon: soon.

Antediluvian: from the time before the biblical Flood; a long, long time ago.

Appeasive: given to appeasement rather than to any conflict which might arise from steadfastness of purpose.

Arcane: requiring secret knowledge to be understood; difficult or impossible to understand.

Autistic: from Autism, a disturbance in psychological development in which use of language, reaction to stimuli, interpretation of the world, and the formation of relationships are not fully established and follow unusual patterns.

Barratry: the illegal action of persistently bringing lawsuits for little or no reason.

Begat: brought about; caused.

Bentley Subglacial Trench: an area of Antarctica; the lowest surface point on Earth not actually underwater.

Bond: James Bond, a secret agent who personally stops villains from destroying or taking over the world. Regarded by some to be a fictional character.

Boolean: A form of symbolic logic, which was illustrated by Lewis Carroll in the book *Alice Through the Looking Glass* (George *Boole*, 1815-64).

Byzantine: Impenetrably complex; devious, scheming.

Calculus: a branch of mathematics dealing with the way that relations between certain sets (functions) are affected by very small changes in one of their variables as they approach zero.

Candygram: A 20th century means of prioritizing the communication of messages of great urgency and velocity by affixing to them a delivery of candy.

Coign of Vantage: a good position from which to observe or take action.

Coke: *Coca-Cola,* Earth's most popular beverage. Containing phosphoric acid, among other secret chemicals, it is capable of dissolving protoplasm and even various metals. The Coca-Cola Company has been reported to use Coke to clean their delivery trucks.

Da Man: The victor, the most excellent or superior one who is in charge (e.g., "You Da Man," "You ain't never gonna be Da Man," etc.).

Decoherence: an environmental effect on quantum systems (e.g. that quantum phenomena are influence by their taking place in an "ocean" of background radiation) that is capable of rapidly inducing almost classical behavior by drowning out quantum activity.

Derrida, Jacque: (b. 1930) philosopher who introduced "deconstruction" (1960s), a method of analyzing texts based on the ideas that language is inherently unstable and shifting and that the reader rather than the author is central in determining meaning.

Deus Ex Machina: an improbable character or unconvincing event used to resolve a plot; in ancient Greek and Roman theater, a god introduced to resolve a complicated plot ("God from the machine" – in Greek/Roman theater, the person resolving the plot is lowered to the stage by a mechanical contrivance).

Dirac: One of the most important British Quantum physicists (1902-84).

DOD: Department of Defense – ostensibly in charge of "defending the country," but full definitions are lacking for what is meant by *defense* and *country*.

Dr. Strangelove: An ancient film by Stanley Kubrick regarding nuclear war on Earth. The war is precipitated by a character who attributes his sexual impotence to fluoridation of drinking water, and conceives fluoridation to be a covert attack by Russian communists on the United States. (Note: Fluoridation of drinking water is currently regarded by some as a covert attack on the United States by the United States).

Eigenvector: a vector whose value is not zero, corresponding to the value of a variable in an equation that gives a solution that complies with the conditions that exist at a system's boundaries ("eigenvalue"). One example of an eigenvector is, if a car is going *North at twenty miles per hour*, and one steps on the accelerator to double the speed, the car is now going *North at forty miles per hour*.

Entropic: Tending to decay into disorder over time.

Event Horizon: the theoretical boundary surrounding a black hole, within which gravitational attraction is so great that nothing, not even radiation, can escape because the escape velocity is greater than light.

Ezekiel: A Hebrew priest and prophet who lived in the 6th century B.C. Noted for having seen a "wheel in the sky" and viewed it as a portent. Whether the wheel was a message from God or actually a Flying Saucer has been in dispute amongst various scholars.

Fiat: An arbitrary edict.

Firmament: the sky, considered as an arch.

Flaatu: The oldest robot planet in the universe.

Flying Sponge: the spaceship owned by John Prometheus. It is a variable-hulled spaceship, usually about 400 feet in length. In the attack of the Sonic Invaders the ship was shaped with acoustic sound-absorption surfaces – the newspapers said it looked like a "Flying Sponge", and the name stuck. John Prometheus also liked the name because of the allusion to Jacques Derrida's allusion to French philosophical writer Ponge.

Fundament: the buttocks.

Fusillade: A barrage of gunfire; a sustained attack.

Gambit: In chess, a move which sacrifices pieces or position for some later advantage in the game.

Glossosphere: That sphere of words that surrounds a planet.

Heresy: an opinion or belief that contradicts established religious teaching, especially one that is officially condemned by a religious authority.

Heuristic: arrived at by using trial and error rather than fixed rules; describes a program that modifies itself in response to the user, e.g. a spellchecker. Example: "most instruction manuals for electronic devices inspire a *heuristic* approach to learning the device."

Hie: Go.

Hypermodern: A style of chess using non-traditional deployment of pieces.

Hyperspace: A postulated space "above" Newtonian space, where objects travel faster than lightspeed; where the hyperpeople live.

Hypothesize: to come up with a possible reason why something is the way it is, which is to be subject to verification by experiment.

Inured: rendered immune to something, by means of experience or constant repetition.

Jack: a playing card ranking between a ten and a queen, with a picture of a young man on it; also, a port into which to insert a plug.

John Frum: Mystic figure of a religious society in the island nation of Vanuatu.

LaLaGuardia Spaceport: A former airport in New New York. Due to the extreme hazards posed by rocket and other space propulsion engines, the earlier airport in the middle of the highly populated area of Queenies, New New York was changed to a spaceport, in the same area.

Lamborghini: a really cool Italian sports car.

Lord it up: to act in a superior, masterful, or bullying way toward others

Maddive: having the characteristics of being or making harassed or mentally unstable

Mawkish: sentimental, especially in a contrived or off-putting way.

Membrane: A Brane is a hyperdimensional membrane – just as a superstring is a hyperdimensional line. It is a dimensional boundary layer of sorts. The term "brane" is a play on "membrane." Branes are defined by the number of dimensions. A two-dimensional surface is a two-brane (D2-brane). Three-dimensional space, such as the known physical universe is a three-brane (D3-brane) moving through time. "D" stands for dimension. So a D5-brane is a five dimensional hyper-surface which propagates in time, thus being a six dimensional space-time structure (definition courtesy of M. Alan Kazlev). [Author's note: compare to Euler's polyhedron formula]

Mesmer: Anton Mesmer (1734-1815), a physician and student of early hypnotism as ascribed to "animal magnetism."

Mexican Standoff: a dispute or argument that cannot be won by either side.

Mien: aspect, mood

Misapperception: mistaken idea about something.

Monkey Chess: chess played by moving pieces at random.

Mustsafe: certainly, without a doubt.

Myst: an early Earth computer game which absorbed a lot of time.

Newtonian Space: the universal space in which the mechanics of Newton occur.

Oblivity: a state of a person being unaware, of which others are very aware.

Persephone: a planet whose orbit is far beyond Pluto.

Phalanx: a group of people or objects standing or moving closely together; in Greek history, a group of soldiers that attacks in close formation, protected by their overlapping shields and projecting spears.

P-K4: The traditional opening move in chess, moving the pawn in front of the king forward two spaces. Also the race of chess-playing robots; they also attempt to automate planets, but the results are not excellent.

Poseur: a person who tries to impress others in an affected or assumed way (disapproving usage).

PsychoPolitics: a science of using brainwashing and mental tricks to defeat an enemy populace. First coined by Beria in 1939.

PsychoToxins: drugs or chemicals which poison the mind, such as psychiatric drugs given to schoolchildren in the late 20th and early 21st centuries.

Pugilism: boxing

Quasar: a compact object in space, usually with a large red shift that indicates remoteness, that emits huge amounts of energy, sometimes equal to the energy output of an entire galaxy.

Rankling: causing persistent feelings of bitterness, resentment, or anger.

Recuse: to disqualify somebody from participating in something because of bias or personal interest.

Red-Shift Horizon: a theoretical limit beyond which, because of red-shift of light spectrum due to speed of recession, nothing can be seen.

***Ride of the Walkyrie*:** a musical work by German composer Richard Wagner. This work was referenced as being used by U.S. helicopter gunships to scare Viet Cong in the ancient film *Apocalypse Now*.

Shout-out: a random address to a single person (or specialized group) over broad-scale media channels.

Sicilian Defense: a basic chess opening.

Sikorsky: a brand of helicopter

Sporadic: not occurring continuously but in random bursts.

Spork: *spoon* plus *fork* in the same utensil.

Square Game: the concept of having a computer lay out all possible variables of a problem, with graded probabilities, then executing every possible variation for effectiveness, then using this to reprogram the original computer; computers designing computers without recourse to human opinion or decision. One aspect of square game is that the tremendous speed of computers makes 1 trillion failed computations for 1 workable one viable.

Standing wave: a stationary wave characterized by points of zero vibration and points of maximum vibration, occurring when two waves of equal frequency and intensity traveling in opposite directions combine.

Stochastic: involving or showing random behavior; probabilistic; involving guesswork or conjecture.

Superstring: a hypothetical one-dimensional entity (string) of extremely short length held to be a fundamental component of matter in some theories of elementary particles involving supersymmetry (a type or symmetry that would apply to all elementary particles). One form of Unified Field Theory involves explaining the basic units (quanta) of energy and matter in terms of tiny vibrating loops known as superstrings, which extend into hyperspace.

Tachyon: faster-than-light particle.

Tautological: self-proving; true under all circumstances.

Teracycles: trillions of cycles per second.

Thou: the person being addressed.

Three Laws (of Robotics): originated by famed SF writer Isaac Asimov, the three laws addressed human concerns regarding the power and speed of robots:

1. A robot shall not harm a human being, or through inaction, allow a human being to come to harm.
2. A robot shall obey all orders given to it by a human being, except where this conflicts with the first law.
3. A robot shall protect its own existence, except where this would conflict with the first or second laws.

Thy: belonging to the person being addressed.

Time's Arrow: the aspect of entropic change from lesser to greater randomity as a phenomenon of time, as in the decay of atomic particles. In Quantum Theory, phenomena at the subatomic level do not show which direction time is flowing.

Tort: in civil law, a wrongful act for which damages can be sought by the injured party.

Toto: canine star of the ancient movie *The Wizard of Oz* (1939).

Truncating: shortened by having a part cut off or removed.

Turing: Alan Turing (1912-1954), British Mathematician.

Twinkie: a sponge-cake snack, filled with a whipped-cream material, originated in 20th century Earth. In one notable late 20th century court-case, a murder suspect claimed that he was "not guilty" by virtue of the (psychiatrically-recommended) claim that the extremely high sugar level in the Twinkie was the cause behind him committing the heinous act. This became known as the "Twinkie defense."

Vaunted: boasted about or praised in an ostentatious way.

WarWare: as the Earth was becoming the target of weekly invasions by other races, as well as spontaneous eruptions of mutated life forms resulting from cell phone use, terrorist groups, etc., Jip Psychic found himself in the thankless job of inventing new weapons which would be effective. Having dispatched the troublesome life forms, he would then attempt to inform the now-rescued government, and then, ignored, sell effective weapons through his own company, *Jip Psychic WarWare, Ltd.*

Wassup: a greeting – "what's happening?"

Yon: over there.

Zero: shows that something is *not* there that could/should be there.

Zona Ruja: an area of prostitution in Tijuana, Mexico. *Do not go there.*

***

The Flommy saga continues:

Flommy goes 100 Trillion light-years to the UltraVoid to communicate with the Wave Eternal – and bring back the *Actual* Laws of Robotics!

Queen Fleena explains a *flaw* in the famous Michelson-Morley experiment!

BOXOR and Jip Psychic *together* fight a frightening mutant plague!

John Prometheus and Sgt. Cowboy fight the *CyBots* in the underground maze of planet Neft!

Wendy discovers an unexpected *dark side* to robot civilization, as well as herself…

Buy the next book in the incredible Flommy series!

FLOMMY THE ROBOT 2: *ON THE EDGE OF BEYOND*

By Daniel Robinson

About the author

Dan Robinson was born in Tuscaloosa, Alabama in 1959. He grew up in a military family and lived in many places. He studied music composition and poetry at the University of Alabama and graduate studies in Music and English at State University of New York at Stony Brook.

Dan lives in New Jersey with his wife, Maria.

He drinks Coca-Cola.

This is his first published novel.